# Buffalo
## *Soul Lifters*

# A Homespun Collection
# of Inspirational Stories

*by*
*Frank Thomas Croisdale*

*Photo montage on cover:*
(*Top, left-to-right*) The Kelly Family, photo from Hunter's Hope; Pope John Paul II, photo from Hope For Tomorrow; (*left, middle*) Teddy Schwytzer, photo from Carlton Studio; Firefighter Brain LaRock, photo from Frank Croisdale (*right, middle*) Carly Collard, photo by Jim Bush; Irv Weinstein, photo by Bill Dyviniak for The Buffalo News; (*bottom*) restored carousel pony, photo from Hershell Carrousel Factory; Father Baker, photo from Our Lady of Victory Institutions; Roger Woodward, photo from Roger Woodward.

©2004 Western New York Wares Inc.
All rights reserved.
Printed by Petit Printing
Layout and Design by Gracie Mae Productions

Address all inquiries to:

**Brian Meyer, Publisher**
Western New York Wares Inc.
P.O. Box 733
Ellicott Station
Buffalo, NY 14205

e-mail: buffalobooks@att.net
Web site: www.buffalobooks.com

This book was published and printed in Buffalo, NY
ISBN: 1-879201-48-8

**Visit our Internet Site at
www.buffalobooks.com**

# Contents

# Contents

# *Acknowledgements/Dedication*

There are many people without whose help the completion of this book would not have been possible. They have all been purple balloons in my life and I am thankful for their aid and assistance in bringing this concept to fruition.

- Lisa Donato of Hunter's Hope was most helpful in arranging the interview with the Kellys and in getting me all of the background information needed to fully understand the miracle that is Hunter Kelly.

- Coach Rob Milligan of the Pavilion Central School District was the cog that drove both the Teddy Schwytzer and the John Clary stories contained in this collection. The kids of Pavilion are blessed to have a coach and teacher who gives so much of himself on a daily basis.

- Kathy and John Chimento, owners of the Red Carpet Motel in Niagara Falls, were kind enough to supply, free of charge, a room where a writer could find a quiet space to think and to write. As I was writing these pages, my family and I were in the process of packing to move into our new home and the Chimentos kind gesture was most appreciated.

- It is said that some of the best friends you'll ever make, you make as a child. John Breed has been my friend since I was 12 years old and the Niagara Falls Firefighter was most kind in helping me secure interviews with fellow firefighters Gary Carella and Bill Butski. Thanks, John.

- The story concerning the bond between a Jewish Merchant and a Catholic Priest that saved Niagara University is little more than a rewrite of research done by Niagara Falls resident Karen Hasley for a stage play that she plans on writing concerning the benevolent gesture. It is used here with her permission and I'll be first in line to buy a ticket when her play makes it to the stage.

- Just as all of Hollywood is connected within six steps of Kevin Bacon, Western New York can be linked through the Six Degrees of Rick Winter. My ubiquitous friend was most helpful in arranging interviews with many of the subjects contained within these pages and has my eternal thanks.

- The day that I married my wife I gained not only a soul mate, but a wonderful second family as well. My brother-in-law Rick Colern helped me secure the interview with the Deubell family detailed inside. My love of language leads me to the realization that brother-in-law = friend-indeed.

- You're lucky if during your school years you cross the path of a skilled and caring teacher. If that teacher happens to become your friend when you reach adulthood, your luck is upgraded to a blessing. Paul Gromosiak was my earth science teacher in junior high school. The author of numerous books concerning Niagara Falls, published by Buffalo Books, continues to mentor me both in his words and with his deeds. His support of my creative endeavors has never wavered and my admiration for this gentle man of nature continues to grow.

*I dedicate this book to two very special people:*

No one has a resume quite like Mike Hudson. Lead singer for the influential punk rock band "The Pagans," book reviewer for the Irish Echo and Editor-in-Chief for the best small-town newspaper in America, the Niagara Falls Reporter. Mike certainly didn't take the traditional route to success and the world's a better place because of it.

Mike runs a newspaper the way that one should be run; he cares about exposing fraud and liberating truth. Mike has a passion that bleeds from every pore in his body and woe be unto you should you cross him the wrong way.

What has never been discussed in print is the fact that Mike displays passionate devotion to his friends in the same measure that he doles out venom for his enemies. His loyalty to those he cares about speaks directly to the fierce heart beating inside of this funny, creative, intelligent and devoted man.

Mike Hudson took a chance on an unpublished and unknown author and for that gesture alone I will forever be in his debt. I attempt to repay that faith each week on the pages of the Reporter and will continue to do so as long as my keyboard keeps spitting out words.

Thanks, Mike, you're a real boon companion.

Every word that you will read in this book carries the scent of my wife Dawn. She is the person who keeps me focused and organized. She's my sounding board and my voice of reason. She's my typist and my proofreader. She edits and she nudges and she coaxes and sometimes she has to plain out shove me in the right direction to make a story whole and complete.

She's my heart and my soul and the perfect mother to our son, Ryan.

The final chapter in this book speaks of the love that I have for my wife. I can do no better in the small space provided here, so I'll let that chapter stand as my public testimony to the woman I love and cherish.

I often chide Dawn by telling her that she won the marital lottery when she married me. It's a kidding that she takes in good jest. The truth is that someone did win the lottery on the day that we were married and I'll always keep that winning ticket in the breast pocket of my shirt – right next to my heart.

I've dedicated my life to being the husband of the former Dawn Colern and I dedicate the words on these pages to her as well.

# *Publisher's Ponderings*

*"Coincidences are God's way of remaining anonymous."*

I remember reading this French proverb years ago. But I only came to understand its meaning in 2003 when two unrelated events collided.

A stranger named Frank Thomas Croisdale contacted me about publishing a book that focuses on inspirational stories in Western New York. It was a topic that strayed far from our publishing company's niches. We're known for marketing books about local history, politics, sports, nature and even haunted sites. But we had never dabbled in the "Chicken Soup for the Soul" genre. Candidly, we never thought about venturing into this new niche prior to Frank's call.

Something strange happened on that spring night as we sat in a booth at Denny's Restaurant on Niagara Falls Boulevard. Frank sold me on the concept. I suspect it surprised me more than it surprised him when I immediately accepted *Buffalo Soul Lifters* as our 2004 publishing project.

Ten days after the meeting, I received a horrifying call. One of my best friends suffered a seizure in Florida as he and his girlfriend were driving to dinner. Doctors discovered a tumor on his brain.

A week later, Lawrence Peita returned to the Buffalo area and underwent surgery and treatment at Roswell Park Cancer Institute. He was only 35 when he was diagnosed with an aggressive form of brain cancer.

Throughout the next 16 months, it was an almost surreal situation.
I was working on our first publishing project that focused on local acts of bravery, kindness and fellowship at the same snapshot in time when I was witnessing the goodness of the human spirit through Lawrence's valiant struggles.

We were putting the finishing touches on the book you're holding now just as my buddy was transitioning into his life at The Center for Hospice & Palliative Care on Como Park Boulevard in Cheektowaga.

A mere coincidence? I choose to think not.

During my many visits to Hospice House, I've witnessed the magic that many "soul lifters" bring to the lives of Lawrence and other residents.

His loving family and close friends who have done everything possible to make these times easier for him.

Amazing nurses who never seem to lose their patience or their sense of humors. Some spend their breaks chatting with residents or even pop in for a quick visit on their days off, occasionally clutching their kids or a special snack.

Then there are the volunteers who fill the kitchen with the delightful aroma of fresh-baked muffins and cupcakes. Others arrive with colorful floral bouquets, stuffed animals or uplifting words of encouragement.

My most enriching encounters have been sharing smiles and "hellos" with the residents at Hospice. People like Billy who, on his better days, would sit on the patio in his wheelchair, watching a pesky squirrel struggling to steal food from a nearby bird feeder. Or Julia, whose enthusiasm for simple pleasures like a jaunt to the nearby Friendly Ice Cream Shop is contagious. Or Ed, whose recollections about his aviation adventures fuel lively discussion. Or David, who can be seen each day caring for plants or helping with routine chores, or Jean, who can always be counted on to deliver a cherry greeting.

And my friend, Lawrence. Hearing him chuckle is the highlight of my day.

As I write this entry in August of 2004, some days have been more difficult than others for Lawrence. He sometimes has a tough time talking. But words aren't always needed. His eyes never stop talking.

Lawrence, you will always be a soul lifter in my book. I'm so proud to call you my friend.

Brian Meyer
August, 2004

# *Introduction*

**I**It began with a simple purple balloon.

A little girl released a balloon in Utah. Four days later, a newspaper columnist found its remains lying next to a creek nearly 2,000 miles away. That the Guinness Book Of Records lists no other record of any ordinary balloon traveling such a distance comes as no great surprise, because what this book is attempting to chronicle cannot be measured using traditional methods.

After finding the remnants of Whitney's balloon, which you'll read about in chapter one, I decided to begin a quest to find other "purple balloons" in our community. I use the purple balloon as a euphemism for people and organizations that have done something out of the ordinary that stimulate the mind and warm the heart.

Some of the things that you will read about will tempt you to classify them as miracles. Quite possibly they are. But if they aren't, if they fit in a category belonging to man and not God, it in no way diminishes their impact and their importance.

Researching and writing this book has affected me in many very profound ways. Writing a column for a weekly newspaper, I've found that my focus has tended to be on the negative. After all, it's bad news – war, greed, corruption and crime – that drive the circulation of any American newspaper. Sometimes it's difficult not to join in with the doomsayers who think that the end of the world is just around the corner.

What I've discovered is that Western New York is filled with a bevy of wonderful, creative and joyous people who offer purple balloons to their fellow man each and every day. Maybe it's the bad economy or the long, cold winters, or possibly even the Super Bowl losses and Johnny Carson's decades-old shot at us during his nightly monologue. Whatever the reasons, we have become a community of caring folks that take care of one another.

I've always been proud to be from the Niagara Frontier, but never more so than the day that I typed the final words for this book. The collection of people that you are about to meet will awe and inspire you. You've probably heard some of the stories. Others will be introducing themselves to you for the first time. With the exception of the handful of chapters that originally appeared as columns in the Niagara Falls Reporter, everything that you are about to read was written as the result of firsthand interviews that I conducted with the particular subjects of each story.

My hope is that along with providing an enjoyable read, the stories contained herein will inspire you to become more involved with this wonderful community we call home. Many of the chapters contain contact information to learn more about the people and organizations profiled. If one in particular catches your fancy, I encourage you to contact them and donate your time or resources.

For me, what began with one purple balloon has turned into dozens. I am so very proud to live in the same community as the people in this book. They have all touched my heart and lifted my soul and I am forever enriched for having made their acquaintance.

May a purple balloon float into your life just when you need it the most.

# *Flight Of Purple Balloon Proves That Miracles Exist*

*The balloon seems to stand still in the air while the earth flies past underneath.*
– Alberto Santos-Dumont

**D**ear Whitney:

Do you believe in miracles?

Before you answer, let me tell you that many adults do not. Most of them did when they were your age, but life's trials and tribulations have a way of stealing the power of belief from even the heartiest of souls. It's probably not even fair of me to ask such a question of one as young as you, Whitney. After all, chances are you're still struggling with mastering the rules of spelling. Rules that teach you things like it's "I" before "E," except after "C," then confuse you with sufficiently weird exceptions like "sufficiently" and "weird."

But ask it I must, Whitney, because if there were any doubts in your mind that miracles do indeed exist, the events of last week most assuredly laid them to rest. Before I go any further, let's clarify right here and now, Whitney, that the reason that many adults no longer believe in miracles is because they look for them at the wrong times and in the wrong places. Many people only seek miracles when they're at the end of their rope. They only choose to believe when they've exhausted all other resources and only a miracle will save the day. Often, that is too late in the game to seek divine intervention. Still others think that a miracle can only happen in preordained spots, like in a church or synagogue. Of course, you and I know that type of thinking is nothing but a bunch of hogwash, don't we Whitney? A simple purple balloon is all the proof we need that magic can and indeed does happen – the type that can connect Farr West, Utah and Niagara Falls, New York in a way previously unimaginable.

I'm sure that when you awoke on the morning of Wednesday, October 30, it felt just like any other day to you Whitney. Your Dad, William Raymond, got you and your two sisters out of bed and ready for school. Your town of Farr West is approximately 31 miles from Salt Lake City. According to the last census, 701 families and a total of 2,178 people call Farr West home. Your school was founded in 1984 and has kindergarten through 6th grade classes. There are 480 kids who attend Farr West Elementary and you and your sisters are some of the newest, as your Dad just bought a home in town. Your thoughts were probably preoccupied with Halloween and trick or treating that Wednesday, but you were about to set into motion a sequence of events that would prove sweeter than a thousand Halloween goodies.

That day your school was celebrating "Red Ribbon" day. The kids at your school chose "The dream begins with me" as your "Red Ribbon" theme. It was decided that each Farr West Elementary student would set free a helium-filled balloon with an attached tag that read "I pledge to be drug and violence free!" The balloon launch had originally been set for that Monday, but high winds caused it to be postponed. As it was, Whitney, your principal, Mrs. Cutler, silently worried that the rainy and cold weather on Wednesday would prevent the balloons from traveling very far – as it turned out, she needn't have worried at all.

*(Courtesy of Whitney Raymond)*
**Whitney Raymond.**

Some kids tied their balloons together so that they could see them from the ground for a longer period of time before they disappeared into the gray horizon. You decided to launch your balloon solo, Whitney. You watched excitedly from the school courtyard as your purple balloon, decorated with a peace symbol, rose high into the crisp, autumn air. Higher and higher it climbed, until it was but a small dot in the sky over Utah. Soon it disappeared from view completely – as had the other balloons launched by your classmates – and you headed back into school for another day spent conjugating verbs and tackling long division. The story may have come to and end there, but as we now know, this was a day for miracles.

I'll bet that you didn't know, Whitney, that your school has been setting balloons free for many years in a row now. According to Mrs. Cutler, the furthest that one had ever been found was in Wyoming, which is just one state removed from Utah. That's a mere trip around the block compared to the journey your balloon took.

Did I mention that I have a dog, Whitney? Her name is Sydney and – as it turned out - she had a pretty important role to play in this miracle. Sydney is part Border Collie and part Grizzly Bear. Well, she might not actually be part bear, but she weights 87 pounds, so the half of her that's not Border Collie definitely came from something really big. Despite her size, Sydney has a heart full of love and there is nothing that she would rather do than to take me on my daily walk. The morning of Sunday, November 3 was no different as Sydney dragged me through the grass along the banks of Hyde Park Creek, which runs through the center of Niagara Falls.

Now it has never made much sense to Sydney to walk on the sidewalk of the park when there is so much more to see and smell in the grass at the water's edge. At her size, I don't generally argue with her, Whitney, though in this case I must admit that I agree with her wholeheartedly. Walking along the creek, we've seen Canadian Geese make the most graceful water landings, we've watched snapping turtles wait patiently to scoop up an unsuspecting sunfish, we've seen muskrats leave a type of vapor-trail as they jetted out into the creek and we've watched a hundred or more catfish bob at the top of the water at sunrise – almost as if to mock the fishermen who spend all day trying to hook them with all sorts of fancy store-bought lures.

It was as we were walking along the creek's banks behind the city wading pool that Sydney spotted the remnants of your balloon. As she pulled me toward it, I decided that I should pick it up so that none of the geese would swallow it as a mid-morning snack. I remembered that the Aquarium here in Niagara Falls used to have an exhibit that showed all of the items swallowed by a dolphin – among them was a balloon. When I saw that there was a tag on the balloon, I thought that it must be from Gaskill Middle School, which is adjacent to the creek. As I read what was written on the tag I was flabbergasted. Utah! This balloon had been released in Utah, wow. When Sydney and I made it home, I told my wife that I had just taken a most fortuitous walk – I'd gotten my morning exercise and a great story for the newspaper all in one shot.

After I found the telephone number to your school, Whitney – and learned that the school is technically in the town of Ogden, Utah to boot – I called a Mr. Don Paul to ask him about the flight of your balloon. Mr. Paul is a meteorologist for the CBS affiliate in Buffalo, New York, which is just a fancy way of saying that he knows a whole lot about the weather outside. When I told Mr. Paul where your balloon had come from, he couldn't believe it. He asked me more than once if it was an ordinary balloon. He said that the weather service regularly releases special balloons that are designed to travel hundreds

*(Courtesy of Dawn Croisdale)*
**Remnants of Whitney's purple balloon**

of miles, but they are much thicker than regular balloons so that they can float at very high altitudes. Mr. Paul said that for a regular balloon to travel as far as yours' did was "extraordinary."

Speaking of miles, Whitney, I used a computer program to determine the number of miles between Farr West, Utah and Niagara Falls, New York. It turns out that there are 1,913 miles between your home and mine. If you were to make the trip by car, it would take you 30 hours, and 21 minutes. Considering that most people only drive for eight hours per day when they go on a long trip, it would take them over three days of driving to make the same journey that your balloon made on its own.

And what a trip your balloon made, Whitney. Mr. Paul told me that the balloon must have caught the northern branch of the jet stream. If you could have gone along with it, Whitney, you would have seen the most beautiful of sights. You would have looked down on the Black Hills of South Dakota. You would have floated above the Mississippi River and the dairy lands of Wisconsin. You probably would have crossed the Great Lakes of Huron and Michigan and even traversed into Canada before swooping down into Western New York. Most amazingly, Whitney is the fact that you would have steered that balloon to a landing just west of Hyde Park Creek to probably the only place that a newspaper columnist's best friend would have found it on an early November morn.

In a few years, your teachers at school will talk about the word "symbolism," Whitney. If something is "symbolic," it means that it represents something, which is usually greater than itself – kind of like how the fireworks that we watch on the Fourth of July represent the battles of the Revolutionary War that allowed all Americans to live freely. The balloon that you set free was symbolic, Whitney, and therein lies the miracle of October 30th. When you have a helium-filled balloon you hold on to it tightly – much in the same way that parents hold on to their children. There comes a day when you have to let go of that string and let your balloon go free. There also comes a day when each parent must let their children go to find their own way in the world.

I don't know much about your dad, Whitney, but what I say to you next, I say with complete confidence. He's got a tight hold on three strings; one is connected to you and one to each of your sisters. He holds tightly to those strings, as do all parents to the strings attached to their kids, to protect you from everything bad in the world as long as he can. At the top of the list of the things he wants to protect you from are drugs and violence.

A day will come when you are older when your Dad will have to let go of that string. When he does, he can only hope that the lessons he has taught you and the warnings he has issued will keep you safe from the dangers of violence and drug abuse. He hopes that you will follow the example of your balloon and ride the currents of life to the greatest of heights. There is much inspiration to be drawn from the flight of your balloon, Whitney, the type that can give birth to the kind of miracle that every parent dreams of.

Your Friend,

Frank Thomas Croisdale

# *Niagara Falls Trash Collector*
# *A Treasure To Community*

*A Hero doesn't seek riches, he seeks righteousness*
– Unknown.

John Lambert lived his entire life in the city of Niagara Falls, passing away on June 12, 1997, at the all-too-young age of 58. If the name doesn't ring a bell, don't worry. Johnny didn't socialize much, and he wasn't exactly the master of the first impression, either. You see, John Lambert wasn't a famed politician or a conquering war hero, or even a misguided thrill seeker hiding behind the moniker, "daredevil." No, what Johnny Lambert was, my friends, was a garbage man. He also was my hero.

Johnny was what some people would call slow. I used to think that way myself, now I think it's the rest of us who may be a little slow. With hair that defied the approach of a comb, clothes that were worn for Guinness Record Book lengths of time, and thick fingers that looked like a collection of half smoked stogies, he was the epitome of trash collecting chic.

A man of few words, John Lambert rarely spoke, and when he did, it was only to people he trusted. Why then, you may ask, was he my hero? Johnny Lambert was my hero because he did something that everyone else I have ever met has only fantasized of doing--he fulfilled all of his dreams before he left the planet.

Johnny had two goals in life. The first was to become a garbage man.

How hard can it be to become a trash collector? Considering Johnny's limitations, it was a five-year process. When Johnny first interviewed to become a garbage man with the city of Niagara Falls, he was politely rebuffed and told to reapply again during the next hiring period.

When the next two hiring periods came and went without him being offered a job, Johnny decided to take matters into his own hands. So began the five-year odyssey of Johnny Lambert collecting the refuse of the citizens of the city of Niagara Falls, for FREE!

Every morning at 3:30 a.m., Johnny would rise from bed and walk (Johnny didn't drive, but more about that later) from his home in the 1800 block of Weston Avenue, across town to have a cholesterol-laden breakfast, Johnny didn't count calories, at the Wedge Restaurant.

Sufficiently energized, Johnny then would begin to collect the garbage for an entire route. At first, the compensated trash collectors were somewhat taken aback by Johnny. After all, it's not every day that a private citizen offers to perform your job duties for you. Once they realized he was not a private eye hired by the city to test their work ethic, the garbage men did what countless CEOs before them have done, they put their feet up and turned a buck on another man's sweat equity. Once his route was completed, Johnny put phase two of his plan into motion. He would arrive on the steps of city hall at 8:45 a.m.--Johnny was the world's most efficient trash collector--and await then-Mayor Michael C. O'Laughlin.

"Good morning, Mayor. Got a job for me yet?" Johnny would ask, mantra like, to the befuddled mayor each morning.

*(Courtesy of Frank Croisdale)*

**Johnny Lambert's garbage truck.**

Pretty soon, the mayor got wind of the fact that Johnny already had begun collecting the garbage. What went through the mayor's mind each morning as this little slice of American drama played out on the steps of the city's hub, I cannot say. What I can report to you are the facts as I know them. After five straight years of arriving to work and being confronted by Johnny Lambert sitting on the front steps of city hall, the mayor one day diverted from his stock answer to Johnny's query--which was, "Not today, Johnny," for those of you keeping score at home--and instead responded, "Today's your lucky day, Johnny, come have a seat in my office."

In reality, it was the mayor's lucky day, because that morning he hired the best damn garbage collector the city has ever known.

Having fulfilled his first goal, Johnny then set his sights on his other secret desire, to obtain a driver's license. The first thing Johnny did after applying for his learner's permit was to enroll in a driving school course. Now, if you can close your eyes and imagine Johnny poured into a training vehicle with the instructor and three pimply-faced, brace-flashing, Tommy Hilfiger-attired teen-agers, you may, for the first time in your life, have complete understanding of the phrase "truth is stranger than fiction." Johnny had one small obstacle in his pursuit of a driver's license: he couldn't keep the car straight!

Johnnie's driving style, sharp movements from left to right interspersed with heavy, unnecessary braking, hadn't been seen by the world since Al Pacino's blind character took a Maserati for a spin in *Scent of A Woman*, and quickly prompted the driving school to issue him a full refund on the condition that he never get behind the wheel of an automobile again.

Undaunted, Johnny scheduled his driving test anyway. On the day of his test, Johnny's family fretted over their rosary beads and prayed that both he and the test official made it back alive. Johnny returned from his test, as was his custom, in silence. Two weeks later, a letter arrived from the D.M.V. that contained Johnny's New York State Driver's License.

To this day, there is debate as to how he obtained that license. Was it a computer foul-up? Did he bribe the instructor? Divine intervention? Whatever the real reason, one thing is certain: Johnny Lambert achieved, beyond hope, the second of his lifelong goals.

So the next time your alarm clock rips through the serenity of your dreams, and you awaken to the notion that you just can't stomach the thought of another work day with your nose to the grindstone, take a moment and think about Johnny Lambert and the determination he had to achieve what most of us take for granted.

*Postscript: Johnny Lambert's driving career lasted one day. He took the family car and made it one block, from where he telephoned back home to report that he had hit two parked cars and stranded the vehicle on someone's front lawn. He happily retired his set of car keys, but proudly carried that license with him for the rest of his life. Long may your spirit shine, Johnny.*

# *Son Of Buffalo Bills Great Gives Hope To The World*

*"For I know the plans I have for you," declares the Lord, "plans to prosper you and not to harm you, plans to give you hope and a future."*
–Jeremiah 29:11

Hope may be the most splendid word in the English language. It's what we cling to when all else is lost. It lights the darkened path before us and lets us know that it's safe to lay the next footstep down. It is hope that renders useless the word yield and hope that swirls sweetly around each dream of tomorrow.

The essence of hope has never been captured better than in the words of poet Emily Dickenson:

> *"Hope" is the thing with feathers –*
> *That perches in the soul –*
> *And sings the tune without the words –*
> *And never stops – at all –*

*(Courtesy of Hunter's Hope Organization)*
**Camryn, Hunter and Erin Kelly.**

Hope redeems the phrase "four-lettered word". Hope listens, comforts, and heals. Hope, of course, is what springs eternal.

It is the gift of hope that a seven-year-old Orchard Park boy has given to his family, his community, and to the world.

Hunter James Kelly was born on February 14, 1997 with great expectations for his life. His father Jim, retired Hall of Fame quarterback for the Buffalo Bills, wished for nothing more than a son to toss a football to out in the backyard. Jim dreamed of teaching Hunter to hunt, fish and do the type of "guy" things that he had growing up with his five brothers in East Brady, Pennsylvania. Jill Kelly looked upon her newborn son with the special type of love that's reserved for mothers and their children. Her desire for Hunter was not unlike that of most mothers for their baby boys – to follow his dreams and make them come true. Jill dreamed of helping Hunter reach the highest altitudes while knowing that his tightrope in life would always be surrounded by a safety net woven from a mother's love.

The Kellys had no way of knowing on that joyous Valentine's Day in 1997 that Hunter would exceed those expectations and take all of their lives in directions never imagined.

*(Courtesy of Hunter's Hope Organization)*
**Hunter, Jill, Erin and Camryn Kelly.**

"From the moment that we brought Hunter home from the hospital I knew there was something wrong – he cried all the time," Jill said as she sat at the dining room table of her Orchard Park home on a sunny February morning.

When Hunter was four months old, the Kellys would hear the words from neurologists at Children's Hospital that turned their world upside down. Hunter had Globoid Cell Leukodystrophy, commonly referred to as Krabbe disease. There is no known cure and the disease, which attacks the central and peripheral nervous systems, is fatal.

"They basically told me that there wasn't anything we could do but take him home and make him as comfortable as possible," Jill said. "The truth is that I spent the first 14 months of Hunter's life waiting for him to die."

A fact that's not often discussed is that nearly 80% of marriages, when a special needs child is born, end in divorce. The Kellys were not immune to the strain that Hunter's around-the-clock care put on them.

"I spent a lot of that time in the first year after Hunter's diagnosis being angry at Jim," Jill confided. "I was upset that he wasn't doing what I was doing, which was spending every moment with Hunter. It wasn't until later that I realized that guys handle things differently and that Jim was just coping with things in the best way he knew how."

"She sometimes gets mad at me that I don't cry," Jim confided. "I grew up in a family of boys where if you showed emotion it meant you were weak and it got you a swat on the behind. She has no idea how many times I've broken down over Hunter when I've been alone."

Fortunately for Jill and Jim they were able to draw strength from two very powerful sources – their mothers.

Alice Kelly was always "Mom" to everyone, even when Jim was a child.

"When we played midget football, if some of the kids didn't have clean enough uniforms, she'd take them and wash them," Jim said of the woman he affectionately referred to as St. Alice. "Even during my days with the Bills when we'd have the big post game parties here, guys like Thurman Thomas and Bruce Smith would come in and before they'd even grab a beer, they'd sit down with her at this table and talk over the game."

"Near the end of her life she struggled with emphysema and she would sit in our living room and watch the games. She had her oxygen tanks. When we brought Hunter home from the hospital he had the same exact type of oxygen tank. I think it was my mom's way of showing me that he has the same spirit that she had."

Jill's mom, Jacque Waggoner, played an even more direct role in helping the Kellys deal with Hunter's illness. A very successful businesswoman, she took a leave of absence from her job and immersed herself in research to uncover the best ways to aid Hunter.

*(Courtesy of Hunter's Hope Organization)*

***The Kelly family.***

"If I can be one-half the mother to my kids that my mother has been to me, my children will be very blessed," Jill said. "She is the strongest, smartest person I know. Without her guidance, I'm not sure where we'd be right now."

"Hunter helped me realize that God has a plan for us all, far beyond what we can imagine. I knew that one day Hunter would be in Heaven and that I wanted to be there with him, but I needed to do more than just talk about it," Jill explained.

What the Kellys decided to do was to establish Hunter's Hope - a not-for-profit organization dedicated to raising the awareness of Krabbe disease and to provide funding for the research into finding a cure. To date, the organization has awarded over $3.5 million for Leokodystrophy research and has led the way in helping to raise awareness of cord blood transplants. These procedures involve using leftover blood from a newborn's umbilical cord and placenta to help Krabbe babies generate the white matter crucial to normal nervous system functioning. Since 1996, over 25 children born with Krabbe disease have had their lives saved with this treatment.

Hunter's Hope has helped Krabbe families in another more basic way by giving them an outlet to communicate with others facing the same issues. Before Hunter's Hope was established, many families felt as if they were on an island with nowhere to turn for support.

"We have a symposium every year in Ellicottville," Jim said. "Part of the symposium is a group talk. Usually it is just for the women, but this past year (2003) we had it for the guys. There were about 40 guys gathered around in this big room and we went around and everyone told his story. Almost all of the guys have kids who have Krabbe now or who have passed away from it. Some of the toughest guys there were the ones that broke down the hardest."

Communication is the heartbeat that drives the Hunter's Hope organization. Not only do families with Krabbe babies now have a network of support to draw from, but many who come in contact with the organization are inspired to build bridges to their own children.

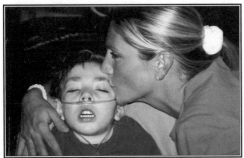

*(Courtesy of Hunter's Hope Organization)*
**Hunter and Jill Kelly.**

"Hunter has inspired so many people to hug their kids and to realize what a blessing they are. Knowing that each day spent with your kids is a miracle. That's what Hunter's Hope is saying to everyone," Jim explained.

The Kellys credit one another for being such good parents for Hunter and their two daughters, Erin and Camryn.

"I've been honored to have been given the 'Father of the Year' award a couple of times," Jim said. "It's my wife that should get all of the awards. I was lucky enough to marry the 'MVP' of mothers. Because of her, my kids are the luckiest kids in the world."

Hunter spends much of his time working with his physical therapists. A handsome young man, he is the spitting image of his father, but the sparkle in his eyes is definitely inherited from his mother.

"Every day there are miracles in our home," Jill said. "Every time Hunter gains a new movement or furthers his ability to communicate, it's a miracle from God."

Hunter is now one of the oldest living persons with Krabbe disease and he continues to amaze his doctors and caregivers. Where the Kellys once feared that Hunter might not celebrate his first birthday, he's now enjoyed seven of them. Each day of his life is a new record and another miracle.

On February 14, 1997, Hunter James Kelly celebrated his own birth by giving the world a giant gift-wrapped box. Inside was a never-ending supply of the world's most precious commodity – hope.

*To learn more about Hunter's Hope contact:*
*Hunter's Hope Foundation, Post Office Box 643*
*Orchard Park, NY 14127, 1-877-984-HOPE, www.huntershope.org*

HUNTER'S HOPE

# Seven-Year Old Boy Survives Plunge Over Niagara Falls Wearing Only Lifejacket

*Impossible situations can become possible miracles*
–Robert H. Schuller

It is known as the "Miracle of Niagara."

On the Saturday afternoon of July 9, 1960, Roger Woodward became the first person to survive a vessel-less plunge over the mighty Niagara. The seven-year-old was swept over the Canadian Horseshoe Falls protected only by a life jacket. Much has been said and written of the events, but little of what has made it to print has revealed that there was more than one miracle that happened on the Niagara River that afternoon.

"It all started with a gesture of kindness," Roger Woodward, now 51, said by telephone from his home in Huntsville, Alabama. "My sister Deanne was about to celebrate her 17th birthday and a gentleman, Jim Honeycutt, who worked with my dad on the construction of the Robert Moses Power Project offered to treat the family to a ride on his boat. Being a low-income family, struggling to survive, the offer was met with great delight by my parents. Although my mom and dad couldn't make it out for the boat ride, they encouraged my sister and I to go. Mr. Honeycutt offered to have each of us bring a friend along. Thankfully, as it turned out, none of our friends were available at such short notice."

On the morning of July 9th, Honeycutt launched his 12-foot, three-seater, aluminum fishing boat powered by a 7 _ HP outboard motor, with Roger and Deanne Woodward in tow, from a dock behind the Cayuga Mobil Home Park where he was living. Of the three, only Roger had on a life jacket – a condition of his mother's when she granted him permission to go on the boat ride.

"Things started out just fine," Roger explained. "I remember going under the Grand Island Bridge and looking up at it and being amazed, from a 7-year-old's perspective, of just how big it was. After quite a bit of pestering from me, Mr. Honeycutt let me steer, which was a real thrill."

Today – partially as a result of the accident of July 9th, 1960 – most boaters and water enthusiasts on the upper Niagara River use the North Grand Island Bridge as a point of no return. To boat past the bridge is to flirt with the danger of the upper Niagara River rapids and the falls that lie beyond. For that reason, most boaters stay well east of the bridge.
In the summer of 1960, Honeycutt, like many boaters on the river at that time, felt that there was little harm in following the water current west beyond the bridge. It was a decision that he would pay for with his life.

"We saw a shoal with hundreds of seagulls on it," Roger explained. "Under Mr. Honeycutt's guidance, I steered us in for a closer look, the sheer pin on the motor broke when we hit a rock. The engine began screaming and the seagulls, frightened by the noise, all took to flight and were in the air screeching all around us."

It's important to note that as a seven-year-old whose family had relocated to Western New York because of the work being offered at the Power Project, Roger had little knowledge of the geography of the region. He'd heard of Niagara Falls, but had no idea that he was on the river that led to the famous water drop. Neither was he aware of the existence or severity of the raging white water rapids that he would soon be thrown into. Most amazing is the fact that Roger Woodward had never learned how to swim.

*(Courtesy of Roger F. Woodward)*
**Deanne and Roger Woodward in 1960.**

Tragically, we'll never know for sure what thoughts raced through Honeycutt's mind as the small boat neared the dangerous rapids, but his lucid actions and strong commands helped to ensure that Deanne Woodward would celebrate many more birthdays beyond her seventeenth.

"The other life jacket was under Deanne's seat, forward in the boat.  As soon as the motor hit the rock it became much louder; due to there being no torque to the propeller to keep  the engine  at a lower rpm. During all this commotion, the first thing Jim Honeycutt did was command Deanne to get her life jacket on. This was his first thought. There was never a moment's hesitation as to who would get the only remaining life jacket," Roger explained. "Then he shut the engine down, grabbed the oars and began to row. All of this happened so fast. By the time Deanne figured out how to put the life jacket on, she was only able to get one of the clasps connected .We saw a big wave ahead and thought this was going to  capsize us. Water came over the bow and then a larger, second wave actually capsized the  boat."

In the next instant, all three of the boat's passengers were thrown into the violent water of the upper rapids.  Roger had been hit in the head by part of the boat when it flipped and he was slightly disoriented from the blow.

"Deanne had been taught to always stay with a boat if it overturns in the water, and she was able to swim to the boat and grab hold of it. Mr. Honeycutt was with me and for a short time; my life jacket, which was adult sized, was keeping both of us afloat. We hit a big wave and he was separated from me – I never saw him again," said Roger.

Honeycutt was swept over the Horseshoe Falls and died instantly.  Because of his quick actions just before the boat hit the rapids, Deanne at least had a chance for survival. "It wasn't until 34 years later, when we returned to Niagara to film a documentary that I really found out the whole story about Deanne's rescue," Roger confided.  "You see, my parents were never comfortable with all of the exposure and media attention put on the family after the accident. Shortly after it happened, we moved to Coxsackie, NY and then on to Florida. My folks attitude was, 'Let's not talk about it' and even though my sister and I are very close, it became a subject that just wasn't discussed."

What Deanne told Roger some 30-odd years after their shared ordeal were a few facts not reported by newspapers at the time of the accident.

The first was that Deanne's maternal instincts for the safety of her younger brother steered her thinking as she worried more about Roger's safety than her own. She had served as almost a surrogate mother for Roger due to severe illness that had afflicted their own mother as the two were growing up.

Second, was the realization that if she didn't think about herself, she might not make it out of the water alive. Deanne began to swim sideways so as not to fight the current as she made her way towards land.

The third and most powerful fact to come to the surface during Roger and Deanne's discussion was just how dramatic her rescue from the river had actually been.

As Deanne was carried past the Three Sister's Islands and entered the section of the upper rapids where the water becomes it's most volatile, the young woman was screaming for help from anyone on the shoreline.

"Of all of the people at Niagara Falls that day during peak tourist season, only one man, a black man who was a vacationing New Jersey State Policeman by the name of John R. Hayes, stepped forward to help Deanne," Roger said. "You have to remember that it was 1960, and attitudes were much different towards black people, who back then would have been called 'colored', or much worse by some people. Understanding the times and feelings back then, it becomes more significant that out of all the people visiting Goat Island that day, it was this wonderful black man by the name of John Hayes who was the only one to immediately step forward from the crowd."

Just at about the point where Deanne was ready to give in to the exhaustion that she was feeling in every inch of her being and accept her fate at the hands of the raging cataracts ahead, a commanding voice from the shoreline snapped her back to attention.

"Come to me girl, swim to me," Hayes barked.

Years of police training had provided John Hayes with a commanding cadence not to be ignored. Deanne began to dig in and swim hard toward the voice.

"That's it girl, swim to me. Harder, girl, now," Hayes commanded.

Finally, Deanne reached close enough to shore and stuck her hand out towards Hayes. The New Jersey policeman was hanging through the guardrail at Terrapin Point and reached out to grasp Deanne's hand. Because of the wetness of her hand and the speed at which she was traveling, Hayes was unable to hold his grasp. Undaunted, he scrambled to his feet and ran along the shoreline ahead of Deanne. Now, just some 20 feet from the brink of the Horseshoe Falls, he would have one final chance to save the girl's life.

"I was just amazed when Deanne told me that, " Roger explained. "I always thought that he got hold of her on the first try. To have the will and presence of mind to run up ahead and try again just blows me away to this day."

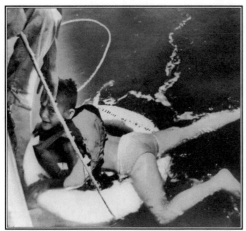

*(Courtesy of Roger F. Woodward)*
**Roger being pulled aboard the Maid of the Mist.**

On the second try, there was no room for error and Hayes succeeded by the slimmest of margins.

"When he stuck his hand out the second time, Deanne fumbled for it and managed to grab on to just his thumb," said Roger.

Hayes began screaming for help and another tourist, John Quattrochi, ran up and grabbed Deanne by the life jacket. The two men were then able to pull the terrified young woman to safety. Deanne's first words to her rescuers speak to the special love shared by the two siblings. "My brother, my brother, he's still in the water," she yelled.

"John Quattrochi realized that I was too far from shore to be rescued and told Deanne to 'just say a prayer' for me," Roger explained. "John Hayes' wife had an 8mm camera and was filming everything. In the movie you see John Quattrochi lean over and whisper something to Deanne, which was, 'just say a prayer', then you see Deanne bring her hands together in prayer in front of herself."

Someone behind the Pearly Gates must have been listening because Deanne's prayers were answered in the most dramatic of fashions.

"Going through the rapids was the worst part of the ordeal. It was like a severe beating that you couldn't make stop. One minute you were underwater, then you were thrown into the air only to slam down into rocks and be plunged back underwater," Roger recalled.

To the horror of stunned onlookers, the boy in the adult life jacket was carried over the Horseshoe Falls to what they thought was a certain death.
"Going over the Falls was like being in a cloud. It was quite peaceful – landing was something all together different. I was plunged into total darkness, I just remember there being pouring water everywhere," Roger told me.

From out of the mist, Roger spotted one of the world famous "Maid of the Mist" tour boats.

"I began yelling and remember becoming disheartened when the boat began to turn away."

In fact, the boat's Captain, Clifford Keach, was actually maneuvering the 60-foot vessel into the best position to bring Roger safely aboard.

"In retrospect, I realize what a tremendous act of seamanship it really was," said Roger.

The crew began to throw a life ring out to the exhausted boy. The first two attempts landed too far away for Roger to grab hold, but the third was a home run. Roger was pulled aboard and, just as Deanne's had been minutes earlier, his first concern was for the well being of his sibling.

"My sister, my sister, you've got to find Deanne," the young boy said to the befuddled crew.

The Woodward kids were taken to separate hospitals, Roger in Canada and Deanne in the United States. They were reunited and the bond that had always been strong between them was further deepened.

Roger, an articulate man who chooses his words with great care and deliberation, looks back on the day that made him famous with mixed emotions.

"First and foremost I'm thankful that Deanne and I are both alive. It does bother me that when the story is told, it's rarely mentioned that Jim Honeycutt lost his life that day – so there was tragedy along with miracles. Also, I had a chance to speak with John Hayes in 1994 and found out that he attempted to visit Deanne in the hospital, but was denied entry. I asked him, 'Why do you think that was, Mr. Hayes?' and he responded, 'Because I was black.' I'm sure that it's quite possible that they were denying admission to anyone that day – I'd like to think that was the reason he was turned away."

Roger also offered his disappointment over the portrayal of John Hayes in the IMAX movie, "Niagara: Miracles, Myths and Magic."

"They contacted me by mail when I was a freshman at the University of Southern Mississippi. I'd never heard of IMAX movies back then as they were just starting out. Influenced by my parents' insistence that we not talk about the accident, I ignored the letter. They made the movie anyway and changed it just enough so that it wasn't specific to me. For instance, the boy in the movie is named "Pete". What really upset me though is that they made the two rescuers white. It's one thing to deny John Hayes his identity, it's another thing all together to deny him his race."

Most importantly, Roger has made it a lifelong habit to distance himself from the many so-called daredevils that willingly tempt fate by challenging Niagara Falls.

"We never asked to be put into that position," Roger explained. "We were just two kids from a poor family looking forward to the gift of a boat ride on a summer afternoon."

Because of the selfless actions of a boat owner giving up the last life jacket to his young passenger, a veteran boat captain displaying superior seamanship and a vacationing police officer reaching across age, racial and safety barriers to clasp a young girl's hand, July 9th, 1960 will forever be known as a day of miracles at Niagara.

*(Courtesy of Roger F. Woodward)*

**Roger in 2004.**

*Roger invites readers to learn more about the Maid of the Mist boat ride:*
*Maid of the Mist Corporation, 151 Buffalo Avenue, Niagara Falls, NY 14303, 716-284-8897,*
*http://www.maidofthemist.com/*

# *Special Friend Leaves Behind A Legacy Of Love*

*Friend, of my infinite dreams
Little enough endures;
Little howe'er it seems,
It is yours, all yours.*
–Arthur Benson

Some things just go together. Peanut butter and jelly. Crayons and a child's imagination. A good book and a shady tree. Chelsea St. Thomas and Goat Island were like that, made to be together.

The first time that she saw Goat Island, it was early fall. She was just a wee thing and her eyes filled with wonder. She couldn't wait to cover every square inch of it.

*(Courtesy of Dawn Croisdale)*

**Goat Island as seen from Canada.**

She loved the sound of the autumn leaves crunching under her feet. She hopped with excitement with each spotting of the indigenous squirrels that came to visit in hopes of a contribution to the winter food-storage drive. She loved the broad, grassy area adjacent to the back parking lot where she would run as fast as her little legs could carry her, until she flopped down in the browning grass trying to catch her breath.

She also loved the symphony of sound conducted by Mother Nature around the isle. The high woodwind wail of the soaring gulls, the driving percussion courtesy of a laboring woodpecker, the deep bass of the falls themselves as their echo resonated off the lower gorge wall, the free-styling jazz scat of a love-drunk chickadee, all backed by a tight chorus of melancholy crickets.

Yes, she loved all of these things, but she loved something else on Goat Island even more: the people. And the people loved her.

I don't know if such records are kept, but I'll state right here and now that Chelsea St. Thomas was probably Niagara's most photographed citizen.

Maybe it was her cheerful face or easy disposition. Maybe it was her deep soulful eyes. Or maybe it was a combination of these things.

But whatever the case, just like a Hollywood movie star, people wanted to be photographed with Chelsea St. Thomas. She was Marilyn Monroe, Madonna and Mae West all rolled into one. Classy, brassy and sassy. She never shied away from a photo opportunity. From cattle ranchers to stockbrokers, sailors to lawyers, office workers to officers of the law, everyone was drawn to her. They asked to have their pictures taken with her on Three Sisters Islands and Luna Island, at Terrapin Point and Prospect Point and in front of the Viewmobile. Some shook her hand, but most dispensed with such formalities and wrapped their arms around her, basking in the positive energy that she emitted.

Not everyone who came in contact with her walked in with a smile, but they all left with one (and not a quick-fading smile, either, but a day long gob-stopper of an ear-to-ear grin).

But to me, she was more than a mini-celebrity; she was a friend. It has been said that you can count the number of true friends you make in a lifetime on one hand. Had I never made another friend in all my years than Chelsea St. Thomas, I would have died a blessed man.

If you were to sit and list the qualities you want in a friend, what words would stare back at you from the page? Loyal, compassionate, brave, trustworthy, non-judgmental, loving, fun?

Chelsea was all of these, and then some. She gave of herself unconditionally. She always had time to spend with a friend. She was a good listener.

I've been accused of being a hopeless optimist. I learned much of that optimism from Chelsea. She always refused to waste one of life's precious moments in a state of worry or despair.

Now, don't get me wrong. She wasn't perfect. There were times when she could be stubborn. She loved the rain, but hated thunder. While most Americans look forward to the Fourth of July, Chelsea was happy to see the fifth arrive. And like any true Western New Yorker, you did not dare lay a finger on her chicken wings. Nevertheless, these were minor faults and, truth be told, her idiosyncrasies simply served to make her more endearing.

In her later years, her time spent on the Island decreased as her health worsened. Bad hips made what was once an effortless, brisk walk around the island a laborious chore. She still loved to greet the world as they came one by one to her corner of the big blue marble, but she knew she had no more to give to an island that she loved so much.

The last time we walked the island together, we stopped and sat, as we had done so many times before, by the current of water just above Luna Island leading to the Bridal Veil Falls. There were no words between us. Our connection transcended words, and we said goodbye the only way we knew how - just two old friends watching the sunset while the raging river washed away my tears.

She passed a week later. The fish wraps did not report her death. This would have made her happy, as the only use she had for newspapers is not fit for public discussion.

She was cremated.

*(Courtesy of Dawn Croisdale)*

*Luna Island.*

On a cloudy and cold spring morning, my wife Dawn and I took her ashes to the island and scattered them at her favorite greeting place near the entrance to Three Sisters Islands. A smattering of early season tourists milled about. Moments later, a ray of sunshine burst through the gray sky and drew everyone's eyes heavenward. Chelsea St. Thomas was on the job.

Chelsea St. Thomas Croisdale was an Old English Sheepdog and truly man's best friend.

# *Amherst Surgeon Gives Kids From Impoverished Countries Something To Smile About*

*A shining isle in a stormy sea,*
*We seek it ever with smiles and sighs;*
*To-day is sad. In the bland To-be,*
*Serene and lovely To-morrow lies.*
–Mary Clemmer

**W**hen you hear the phrase "plastic surgery," what images spring to mind? For many, the words conjure up thoughts of well-to-do, middle-aged women battling the inevitable effects of aging by lifting chins, fattening lips and tucking tummies.

There is another, altruistic, side of the practice. Often plastic surgeons are called upon to help folks that have been disfigured, by birth or by accident, and aid them in regaining a sense of confidence by feeling good about their appearance.

One might associate plastic surgery with the affluent denizens of Amherst, New York, but surely not poverty-stricken towns in Russia, Cuba, India and Poland. And who – even those predisposed to dreaming impossible dreams – would imagine a connection between plastic surgery, Mother Teresa and Pope John Paul II?

Fortunately, this book is about Western New York and the special people who live here. There is probably nowhere else in America where the dots that I've outlined could be connected, but connected they are. Let me introduce you to Board Certified plastic surgeon Dr. Jeffrey Meilman.

Speaking from the conference room at his Maple Road offices in Amherst, Dr. Meilman was the portrait of the genteel medical professional as he explained how the organization with which he is so closely associated – the Hope For Tomorrow Foundation – got its start.

"I started doing some medical work abroad in 1991," Dr. Meilman said. "I realized that there were many people in impoverished nations that were in need of reconstructive surgery. Many of my clients are well-to-do women who enjoy the benefits of cosmetic surgery. As I became friends with these ladies, many of them were saying that they felt blessed to have privileges that others didn't and wanted to do something to give back. I told them of my experiences helping people overseas and the idea for Hope For Tomorrow began to take shape."

As luck would have it, a papal visit for about 30 Western New Yorkers was being arranged. The ladies decided to run the idea of Hope For Tomorrow by Pope John Paul II.

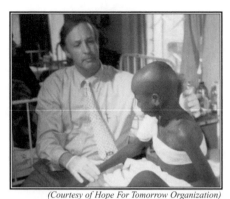

*(Courtesy of Hope For Tomorrow Organization)*
**Dr. Meilman with a patient in India.**

"They had a good 30 minute audience with the Pope, who listened politely to their idea," Dr. Meilman said. "When they were done he told them that it was a splendid concept and gave it his blessing. So in 1994, Hope For Tomorrow was officially launched."

The group got started by having a fund raising dinner for the people of the community. The idea was to judge the support level of what they intended on doing.

"The first year we did well. The next couple of years not so great, but since 1996, we've done exceptionally well. We usually average 500 people at $100 a plate," Dr. Meilman said.

The group customarily makes two trips per year to an impoverished country, where multiple surgeries are performed.

"The ladies and men that come with us pay their own way. They assist in the surgeries as often we're operating in the bush. We bring extra medical supplies to leave with the hospital that we are working with," he explained.

Often, the group will encounter a child that is too badly injured to be safely operated on in the field. In those cases, the child is flown back to Buffalo to undergo surgery at an area hospital.

"Usually, three or four kids per year are brought back to Buffalo. A parent and sometimes siblings will accompany them. The members of the organization arrange for their care while they're here. Once the surgery is completed, we monitor them until they have fully recovered and get them back on an airplane headed for home," said Dr. Meilman.

Most of the kids who are operated on have facial deformities and there is no doubt that the surgery provides them with a dramatic increase in self-esteem.

Once the surgeries are completed, the Vatican is notified. Pope John Paul II has made it a standing policy, whenever it can be arranged, to meet with the child and his or her family and offer his blessings. Dr. Meilman tells of an incident that took place in Poland when the Pope demonstrated his appreciation of the work that the Buffalo contingent has performed for the benefit of children in need.

"We knew that the Pope was in town visiting and we approached the Archbishop and asked if we could meet with the Holy Father while he was there. 'Absolutely not,' he says. 'This is our chance to meet with the Pope, you can meet him back in America.' We tried another high official who told us the same thing. We found out what route the Pope-mobile was traveling and our 20-member delegation lined the roadside, each holding a little American flag.

The two church officials that turned us down were riding with the Pope. The Pope looks out and recognizes me and two other fellows and says 'Buffalo. Stop, Buffalo!' He made them stop and came over and greeted us all. The two church officials were fuming."

A group of doctors specializing in many disciplines usually accompanies Dr. Meilman on the missions. Conditions are oftentimes far removed from what the doctors have come to expect back in Buffalo.

*(Courtesy of Hope For Tomorrow Organization)*
**Pope John Paul II blessing Hope for Tomorrow patient in 2001.**

"Once we were in Cuba and the doctor there was showing me how he gets the patient prepared for surgery. He gave me a bar of soap and I'm washing my hands and he tells me not to put the soap down when I was through, but hand it to the nurse that was standing next to us. The nurse then took the soap to another doctor who was getting prepped for operation. It was the only bar of soap in the entire hospital," Dr. Meilman said.

One of the toughest aspects of the trips is deciding what children are to be operated on. Much like the judges on "American Idol," the doctors assess all who are presented and make difficult cuts before the first scalpel is raised.

"We try to work on the ones that need no more than an hour's worth of operating time. Otherwise, we'd never be able to get it all done. The severe ones are often flown back for more detailed surgery," he explained. Before her death in 1997, Mother Teresa worked closely with the organization and aided it in assisting the children of Calcutta.

At the time of this writing, the group is planning a trip to Bosnia (in June 2004) to aid the children of that war-ravaged country. Safety for the workers of Hope For Tomorrow is always a concern when the trips are made. Only once has the group turned down the request to visit a nation.

"We were invited to visit Afghanistan not too long after September 11th," Dr. Meilman said. "We felt that it was just too dangerous a country to visit at that time."

A group of ladies from Amherst and a plastic surgeon with a heart of gold have made a huge impact on the lives of countless numbers of children from around the globe. Because of their vision and dedication in seeing it to fruition, those kids have received a gift priceless in nature – they now have hope for tomorrow.

*To learn more about the Hope For Tomorrow Foundation, contact:*
*Hope For Tomorrow Foundation, 811 Maple Road Williamsville, NY 14221, 716-204-0941,*
*www.hopefortomorrowfoundation.com*

# *Couple Sells Everything And The Kitchen Sink To Aid The People Of A South Buffalo Community*

*Work as if everything depends on you and pray as if everything depends on God.*
–Father Joseph Bayne

How a couple first meets usually has little bearing on what the future holds in store for them.

In the case of Gary and Linda Tatu, the place where they first laid eyes on each other perfectly foreshadowed the incredible ups and downs that they would survive in turning a decrepit church on Buffalo's south side into a beautifully renovated building dedicated to helping those most in need.

Gary and Linda met on a roller coaster. Thankfully, it is a ride that they've never really gotten off.

In September of 1992, Gary was thumbing through a real estate multiple listings book when something curious caught his eye. A self-employed building contractor, Gary dreamed of buying a fixer-upper apartment building as a way to ensure financial security when he and his bride reached retirement age. Instead of an apartment building, it was a church, one almost exactly 10 times the size of the Tatu's Williamsville home, that piqued Gary's interest.

A night later, Gary and Linda went to hear Christian singer John Michael Talbot in concert. Talbot did a lot of talking from the stage and reiterated a biblical theme over and over. "Sell all you have, give to the poor and follow me." The Tatus felt like they were at a command performance for an audience of two.

After looking at the Seneca Street church together, and seeing what deplorable condition it was in, Gary and Linda decided to put the decision of whether they should buy the church in God's hands.

"We had all of our money, almost $90,000, tied up into a MasterCard that we'd used to buy a handyman special house and fix it up," Gary said. "I decided to do an open house on a Saturday, which no one does, and had put up just a few signs on Sheridan Drive to advertise it. While I was waiting for anyone to show up, I did something I really hadn't done before. I talked to God."

Gary told God that if he and Linda were meant to buy the church they'd have to sell the house first. Every other home they'd fixed up had sold almost immediately, while this one had been on the market for months.

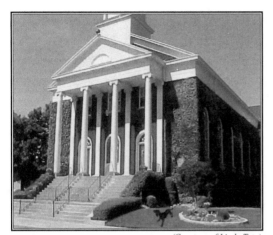

*(Courtesy of Linda Tatu)*

**Harvest House.**

As I detailed in the preface, it was a purple balloon that made its way nearly 2,000 miles that inspired me to seek out the stories contained in this collection. It took God just three minutes to send Gary a purple balloon in response to his plea.

"This guy walks in and says that he wasn't even really out looking at houses, but saw the Open House sign and decided to drop in. After looking around, he said that he liked what he saw and wrote me a check right then and there," Gary explained.

As Gary and Linda seriously looked into the feasibility of buying the church, God kept the purple balloons coming and most of them had the same name - Francis. Everywhere Gary turned, prison retreats, church sermons, even the director of a local soup kitchen, the name Francis, as in St. Francis of Assisi, kept appearing. St. Francis was revered for his commitment to the poor. He gave everything he owned, right down to the clothing on his back, to those who had little. Gary and Linda were about to do the same.

Before we continue, let me ask you a question. What is the best piece of advice that you've ever received? Just about all of us have had someone, at a critical junction in our lives, offer a few words to steer us in the right direction. For Gary and Linda Tatu, that someone was Franciscan Father Joseph Bayne.

After detailing to Father Joe their worries and fears about the monumental task that lay ahead of them, Gary spoke aloud the question that he and Linda had been silently asking themselves.

"How do I know how much I have to do myself, and how much I should leave up to God? Where is the fine line between faith and stupidity?"

Father Joe answered with words that would become the mantra of Gary and Linda for each day forward. "Work as if everything depends on you and pray as if everything depends on God."

After much negotiating, on April 12, 1993, Gary and Linda became the proud owners of the church at 1782 Seneca Street. Linda named the new endeavor Harvest House, where body and soul are nourished.

To finance the massive project that lay before them, Gary and Linda sold their beautiful home in the suburbs and many of their possessions, including Gary's 28-foot boat. The Tatus moved into an apartment inside the church that had once been home to the pastor of the original South Presbyterian Congregation in 1922.

For the first year there wasn't even any heat. The Tatus couldn't afford the approximately $30,000 National Fuel bill that the antiquated heating system racked up annually.

One might think that selling everything one owns and buying a run-down church with plans to restore it, while providing programs to service the community, would be met with cheers of approval and pats on the back, right? Wrong.

"You're crazy," "You've got to be kidding," and "You must be nuts," were phrases hurled at Gary and Linda. And that was from their family and friends.

The South Buffalo community surrounding the church would prove to house many more vocal critics.

"The night that we closed on the building, we pulled up outside and looked at it from our car. Just as we were asking ourselves, 'Well, what are we going to do first?' A police car pulled up behind us. The neighbors had called in because they thought we were casing the place," Linda said.

"Then maybe the third day our next-door neighbor came in our door and came up behind Linda. He was ranting and raving that he wasn't going to put up with this anymore. He scared the living daylights out of her. He was yelling about what a mess the place was. Linda told him, 'We've only been here three days, give me a break.' Two days later, he was circulating petitions at the Senior Citizens Center saying that we were going to attract people that would go in and kill them and that their granddaughters were going to get raped. He scared them so bad, he had over 500 signatures," Gary said.

Welcome to the neighborhood.
Things got so out of hand that councilman Brian Higgins called the Tatus and told them that they had an uprising on their hands. Gary and Linda printed up a slew of flyers and invited the community in for a look for themselves.

The community responded, but it wasn't as the Tatus had hoped it would be. The meeting turned into a screaming session. Gary and Linda couldn't even make themselves heard over the ranting and raving of what quickly was turning into a mob. Finally, the people dispersed, but not before telling Gary and Linda that they'd be back and they'd be brandishing chain-saws. Gary and Linda sat in stunned silence with tears spilling down their cheeks.

"I really didn't know what we were going to do at that point." Linda explained.

Fortunately, the Tatus were about to learn an important lesson. For every rainstorm they would encounter, God would also send a rainbow their way.

Gary walked to the corner delicatessen for the enjoyment of the fresh air as much as for the need of a loaf of bread. Along the way, he was approached by a young girl who asked him if he was the man who owned the church where the meeting had just been held. Gary, who had heard enough from his neighbors at the meeting, was ready to unload his frustration on some-one, anyone, but fortunately he held his tongue.

"It is terrible what those people are trying to do to you," the young girl told Gary. "I am going to pray every day for you for the rest of my life. Don't you dare give up."

That was just the tonic that Gary and Linda needed.

"Now we had a responsibility," Gary explained. "That girl would be watching and we just couldn't go out of business."

Over the next few years the Tatus would be confronted with more obstacles than a horse in a steeplechase competition. Their biggest nemesis was the city, which contended that the Tatus couldn't live in the church because the apartment hadn't been part of the original construction.

*(Courtesy of Linda Tatu)*

**Harvest House chapel.**

After many hearings, Gary and Linda finally went to court and produced a copy of the secretary's minutes from a church meeting in 1923. In the notes it was mentioned that the Pastor had moved into his new living quarters, thereby proving that they were constructed along with the church. The book containing those notes had been given to Gary just hours before the hearing. Gary, while fearing that he would never find definitive proof that the living quarters had been constructed along with the church, had flipped open the book to the exact page with the secretary's minutes. Proof, once again, that an angel was looking over the Tatus.

The couple faced an almost continuous stream of city inspectors, who cited them for one violation or another. Oftentimes, the inspectors contradicted one another, and even them-selves. Things got so ridiculous that an inspector cited the Tatus for allowing guests to park on a gravel parking lot. The offense was a breach of some archaic and non-enforced city law. The inspector noted this infraction on Christmas Day.

The most surreal moment came when a group of teen volunteers from the "Youth Engaged in Service" organization painted the church's dining room. A photographer for The Buffalo News stopped by to take pictures. The newspaper ran a photo of the kids' altruistic effort in the next day's edition. An employee of the Department of Labor soon visited the Tatus. He cited them for violating child labor laws by employing a minor on a construction site. After arguing that the kids were volunteers, not employees, and were just painting a wall for crying out loud, Gary and Linda were let off with a warning.

Despite years of hurdles, the Tatus continued to work as if everything depended on them, while praying as if it was all on God's shoulders. As a result, Harvest House flourished.

Today, Harvest House is home to a thriving baby ministry that provides cribs, car seats, changing tables and clothes to expectant mothers of little means. Over 200 agencies refer pregnant women to the Harvest House ministry. Diverse church groups from all over the country, and many parts of the world, have used Harvest House for their retreats.

Gary and Linda have turned what once was an eyesore into a pristine monument to hard work and perseverance. The church has been transformed into a multi-dimensional facility featuring a chapel, gymnasium, cafeteria and game room. Linda's work in landscaping the grounds outside Harvest House won her first place in the prestigious "Buffalo In Bloom" contest.

The Tatus had often said that there would be no Harvest House II. They had no desire to start the struggle all over again. Ten years, and many lessons learned, have changed that stance. Gary and Linda now have blueprints for the next phase of Harvest House. The new venture will encompass an entire city block, just a couple of miles from Harvest House. The plan is to move the baby ministry to the new building where it will be greatly expanded. In addition, they will partner with many organizations and medical professionals to bring a cornucopia of services to the citizens of Buffalo.

By working as if everything depended on them, and praying as if it all depended on God, Gary and Linda Tatu have made their dream of offering a sanctuary where body and soul are nourished into a reality.

The couple who met on a roller coaster continue to demonstrate their love of God, and their love of their neighbors, by helping so many get back on track.

*To learn more about Harvest House, contact:*
*Harvest House, 1782 Seneca Street, Buffalo, NY 14210, www.harvesthouse.ws*

# *Free Coats, Books and Bread =*
# *One Man's Plan To Save*
# *Buffalo Church*

*The dedicated life is the life worth living. You must give with your whole heart.*
–Annie Dillard

If you could give something back to your community, what would it be? Beyond money, that is. Maybe you'd plant a garden or help erect a playground. Possibly, you might start a community library. Perhaps you'd set up emergency food, laundry and shower facilities. You might even help mentor a child or offer support to someone struggling with the demons of drugs and alcohol.

Whichever way you'd choose to help, it would start by offering the gift of your own time. The story that follows concerns one man's efforts to do just about everything listed above for the people of the Seneca-Babcock community. His name is Brian Rotach and he is the pastor of the 116-year-old Seneca St. United Methodist Church.

"Free coats, books and bread" reads the sign outside the church on the corner of Seneca Street and Imson in the Lovejoy District of Buffalo. When you think about it, what else does a person truly need? A coat to offer protection from the elements, a book to sharpen the mind and a loaf of bread to quell the calls of hunger from the belly. Even Maslow would have to agree that the lower blocks in his hierarchy of needs are all pretty much covered by the sign's promise.

Today, the church serves hundreds of kids and adults with a myriad of outreach programs. So popular is the work done at the church that Daemen College has become a major partner. The college offers dozens of helpers for after school programs. Kids are provided with a hot snack and get help with their school studies.

In the not so distant past, things were not quite so rosy. In fact, you could say they were down right bleak.

"Seneca St. Church should have closed. It was supposed to have closed ten years ago," Pastor Brian explained from his office. "There were only about ten or eleven active members of the church left, and they had spent the last dollar of an endowment, which they'd lived off of for some time, about three months before I got here."

Pastor Brian had been assigned to the church only on a temporary basis, but slowly discovered that he had found his calling and his new home.

*(Courtesy of Seneca St Church)*

**Brian Rotach.**

"This neighborhood (where the church is located) is over 100-years-old and long provided industrial workers from places like Buffalo Anodyne and Republic Steel easy walking distance or a trolley car ride to downtown. When all of these heavy industry jobs left the area, the people here were impacted greatly. Those with finances to leave did, and the rest hung on and did the best that they could as things regressed," Rotach explained.

"Thirty years ago there was an A&P, a police station, a fire station, a public school, a Catholic church and school, a pharmacy, a movie house, a bakery, a greengrocer and several other businesses in this neighborhood. They're all gone now."

What has remained in the once proud neighborhood are a couple of bars, a few businesses and two churches. Single moms head up the households in approximately 90% of the homes in the community of 1,400 people. Most of the ladies have multiple children. Teen pregnancy is common. The average household income is below the national poverty level.

Many pastors might size up the long odds facing a community like Seneca-Babcock and start circling the days left on the calendar of a temporary assignment. Most would probably request to be sent to the safety and prosperity of a suburban congregation, but not Brian.

What swayed him was the conviction displayed by that initial congregation, lacking enough members to field a regulation softball team.

"We began to meet on Thursday nights in addition to Sunday to pray and discuss what God might have in store for us," Brian said. "The members had all but resigned themselves that the church was in its final days, but decided that they wanted to go out with a flourish."

The group decided to host a Sunday school even though the room that had housed one previously, on the 2nd floor of the church, was inaccessible to most of them. One woman suggested that while she couldn't teach, she would cook breakfast for the kids – and so it came to pass.

"We put flyers up around the neighborhood and with the promise of a hot breakfast on Sundays, something not available to most of these kids. We had kids right from day one," said Brian.

That was just the shot of encouragement that the congregation and Pastor Brian needed to realize that their church would not become another boarded-up building in a neighborhood that already housed more than its share.

The Sunday school expanded to include the after-school programs. Soon, kids from kindergarten right through high school, were showing up at the church to improve their lot in life. Pastor Brian bartered, traded and shrewdly negotiated his way for the supplies to establish a lending library, game room, computer lab and gymnasium for the kids to use. In almost all cases, these are privileges that would be lost to the kids if not for their availability at the church.

For many years, Pastor Brian worked at the church only part time. The small congregation could not support a salary for him to live on. A little over two years ago, a feeling that had been dogging him for quite some time, came to the fore in his mind. He belonged at the Seneca St. Church serving the people of Seneca Babcock fulltime. Brian contacted the Bishop asking for her prayers and counsel. The Bishop told him to follow God's call and assigned Brian as the full-time pastor of Seneca St. Church.

But how would he survive with little or no money? Brian soon found out that the Lord does indeed provide for those who provide for themselves.

"Word got out what I was attempting to do and soon checks were coming in from all over Western New York," Brian explained. "Today, because of the generosity of congregations and individuals throughout Erie and Niagara counties, some of whom I don't even know, my entire salary and the program needs are being met. It truly is a Western New York project."

It is amazing to see the smiles break out on the kids' faces as they stream in through the church doors and are greeted by Pastor Brian.

"Many of the single moms in this neighborhood are outnumbered by their children and by their problems. As a result, under-parenting is a very common occurrence. Most of us take the promise of a hot meal for granted, for the kids here it might not be so. Also, most of us can usually find a hug at home when we need it. Some of the kids who come here are strangers to regular hugs and help with homework. We provide these," said Pastor Brian.

Today, there are programs at the church six days a week. Over one hundred kids are on the active participant list. Youth groups from all over the country visit the church to help with summer projects. They draw inspiration from all that's been accomplished at the building that was set to close its doors a decade ago.

Pastor Brian has also set his sights on attempting to help break some of the damaging cycles that plague the neighborhood. Narcotics Anonymous groups meet twice weekly to help those struggling with drug addiction reclaim their lives, while a new program partners with Planned Parenthood to target the problem of teen pregnancy.

Because of the devotion of Pastor Brian and a group of volunteers, kids from an innercity neighborhood where little can be counted on now are assured of a free coat, books and bread.

That and a never-ending supply of love and support.

*To learn more about Seneca St. Church, contact:*
*Seneca St Church (United Methodist), 1218 Seneca Street, Buffalo, NY  14210*
*Email:  SenecaStBuf@aol.com*

# *How Niagara Falls Helped Inspire Our Nation's "Unofficial" National Anthem*

*So it's home again, and home again, America for
me!
My heart is turning home again, and I long to
be
In the land of youth and freedom beyond the
ocean bars,
Where the air is full of sunshine, and the flag is
full of stars.*
–Henry Van Dyke

**P**atriotism has made a dramatic return since terrorists attacked America on September 11, 2001. American flags are harder to come by than "Tickle me Elmo" was a few Christmases ago. People are flying the Stars and Stripes from homes, cars and boats. Standing for the National Anthem is back in style too. So is removing your hat and placing your hand over your heart while its played.

The question is: What song is truly our National Anthem? The "Star-Spangled Banner" was officially voted that title on March 3, 1931, when President Herbert Hoover signed a bill proclaiming it so. But it has been "America The Beautiful", long known as the "Unofficial" National Anthem, to which people have turned to express the red, white and blue sentiments of their hearts during these trying times.

The words to "America The Beautiful" were first published in 1895. The author, Katharine Lee Bates, was a 34-year-old Professor of English at Wellesley College. The pince-nez-wearing, Bates was slow of foot, but not of thought. Her wit was legendary and her energy boundless.

It may come as a surprise to you to learn that our very own Niagara Falls played a significant role in shaping "America The Beautiful."

In June of 1893, Ms. Bates departed from Boston, Massachusetts, on a rail journey that would take her westward across the United States and immortalize her place in history. The next morning the locomotive pulled into Niagara Falls. Bates kept a diary and had a curious habit of condensing the events of her day into a single line. In Lynn Sheer's book, "America The Beautiful – The Stirring True Story Behind Our Nation's Favorite Song" (PublicAffairs Publishing), she notes that Bates preserved the memory of her brief encounter with the mighty cataracts with this entry: The glory and the music of Niagara Falls.

A poem was beginning to form in Katharine Lee Bates' head, one that would become "America The Beautiful." As a precursor to the fabled ode, Bates scratched down a poem expressly about the majesty of Niagara Falls.

Passion of plunging waters, Columnar
mist and glistening rainbow play;
A splendid thrill of glory and of peril

Sherr said of Bates' visit to Niagara, "(Niagara Falls) became a cultural icon, a symbol of the can-do optimism of a nation poised to enter its second full century. That spirit moved Katharine Lee Bates as well, and it helped shape the poem that was developing in her mind."

*(Courtesy of Wellesley College Archives, photo by Chas. W. Hearn)*
**Katherine Lee Bates.**

Bates' train trek took her to many of America's top cities. Chicago, Kansas City and Colorado Springs among them. Her stay in Colorado included a three-week summer session teaching at Colorado College. At the end of those three weeks, Katharine Lee Bates and fate collided 14,110 feet above sea level at the top of Pike's Peak.

Bates had joined an excursion of fellow professors in ascending to the top of the famous Rockies summit. Once there, two members of her party fainted, thus Bates' view from Pike's Peak was short-lived. It lasted long enough, however, to cement in her mind the final piece of the jigsaw puzzle that would become "America The Beautiful."

"It was then and there," she later wrote, "as I was looking out over the sea-like expanse of fertile country spreading away so far under those ample skies, that the opening lines of the hymn floated into my mind." O beautiful for halcyon skies, for amber waves of grain.

The poem was first published on July 4, 1895, in the Congregationalist – a weekly church publication in Boston. The poem spread like wildfire and was embraced by Americans far beyond the Commonwealth of Massachusetts.

It was another local connection that helped turn the poem into an anthem. Ms. Bates received word that many people were setting her words to music. Honored, she reworked the poem to make it more musical. The revised version was printed in the Boston Evening Transcript on November 19, 1904. Clergyman Charles A. Barbour of Rochester, New York saw the poem in the transcript and felt that it should be married to a hymn. Barbour enlisted the help of his wife, a trained musician, and set the words to a song by Sam Ward entitled, "Materna." The hymn followed the precise cadence of the lines of the poem and, instantly, an anthem was born.

Many musicians feel that "America The Beautiful" is much better suited for the average voice than is the more intricate "Star-Spangled Banner." Count composer Marvin Hamlisch among them. "Its simple and sweet," Hamlisch told Sheer, "It's that climb up, that jump to America! That gives you a feeling of reaching for something big. It's very relaxed up to that point, and then it just bursts forward."

Former San Francisco Opera soprano and Niagara County resident Maria Fortuna offers a dissenting opinion. She said that while she agrees that "America the Beautiful" is easier to sing unaccompanied, there is something about the "Star Spangled Banner" that, for her, places it in a class unto itself. "It's stirring, noble and grand, as our country is grand," said Fortuna. "When the firemen raised the flag at Ground Zero, while the Anthem played, it was as if they were saying, 'Do what you will to us, but our flag is going to fly.' I get goose pimples whenever I hear the Star-Spangled Banner. No other song has that power."

Many feel that Bates reached across time to console a nation in need with the stirring third verse of the final revised version of the poem, published in 1911.

*O beautiful for heroes proved*
*In liberating strife,*
*Who more than self their country loved,*
*And mercy more than life!*

The debate as to which song best represents itself as being worthy of the title of "America's National Anthem" will probably rage on indefinitely. Let's give the final word to Ms. Fortuna.

"They each represent emotions unique to the American experience. Why can't we have both?"

Indeed.

# *Gasport High School Senior Battles MD While Pursuing Dreams Of College*

*Never, never, never, never give up!*
–Winston Churchill

In many respects, Gregory Wagner is like most high school seniors. He loves video games and spending hours on his computer. He enjoys high school, but is looking forward to college. He has the heart of a boy and the maturity of a young man. In one way, however, Gregory is very different from all of his classmates. He has Duchenne Muscular Dystrophy.

America is a country obsessed with labels. You're black or white, old or young, skinny or fat, gay or straight, rich or poor. We've even created a multitude of forms complete with boxes to check to place you in this category or that. But it's not what Gregory Wagner appears to be on the outside that makes him so special. It's what he is on the inside.

"Gregory was a premature baby and he did just about everything late, crawl, stand up and walk. At the time, I wasn't too concerned," Gregory's mother, Debra explained.

A speech therapist that was working with Gregory suggested that he be tested by a neurologist.

"I went in for a muscle biopsy and that really hurt," Gregory said.

The test results led doctors to diagnose Gregory with MD.

"I was scared, but I was determined to fight it with all that I had."

The Wagner family would soon be dealt another devastating blow. Gregory's younger brother, Nicholas, was also tested. It was found that he, too, suffered from Muscular Dystrophy.

"I used to hear them talking in their room at night about how they were going to find a cure," Debra said.

"We didn't know that you could hear us," Gregory replied.

Gregory was 13 when Nicholas, who was only 11, passed away while awaiting a heart transplant. Due to the close bond between the two brothers, Gregory took Nicholas' death very hard. "I guess I just didn't want to believe it. It wasn't until we went to his funeral that I realized he wasn't gong to be here anymore."

Most people with MD eventually lose the ability to walk. Due to a drug called Prednisone,

Gregory has thus far been able to remain ambulatory. While he uses his wheelchair to navigate the halls at school, he is able to stand and walk short distances with the aid of a walker. The medication that Gregory is on does come with side effects, such as giving his face an unnatural puffiness. Despite those limitations, his sweet smile and twinkling eyes still manage to break through and capture the heart of whomever he is engaging in conversation.

*(Courtesy of Debra Wagner)*

**Gregory and Deborah Wagner.**

One thing that Gregory is most definitely not afflicted with is the lethargy that consumes so many teenagers. He was an active Cub Scout and Boy Scout, where he earned the prestigious rank of Star Scout. Gregory has been actively involved with the MDA telethon each and every year since 1992. He initiated a very successful hop-a-thon, along with an annual Boy Scouts farmers breakfast. Both raise funds for MDA research.

Debra Wagner is a registered nurse at Mt. St. Mary's Hospital in Lewiston and Gregory often goes to work with his mom and serves as a volunteer at the hospital.

"I pretty much do whatever they need me to do, run supplies here and there. I guess I know just about every square inch of the hospital by now," Gregory explained.

When Gregory was 10 years old the Make-A-Wish Foundation extended him an invitation to take a dream vacation. Gregory chose to travel to Seattle, Washington, and visit the headquarters of the Nintendo Corporation. It was a trip that would change his life forever.

"(The Nintendo people) were great to him," Debra said. "They made him honorary 'President for the Day' and gave us a full tour and a bunch of games to take home."

"I knew right then and there that I wanted to be a game designer and that I wanted to work for Nintendo," Gregory stated.

As Gregory made his way through high school, his desire to make a living designing computer games grew stronger. He now had a new dilemma, where would he go to college? For all of the advancements that our country has made over the past two decades in making buildings more handicapped accessible, there still aren't a lot of options available at the collegiate level for a kid with MD.

Fortunately, an angel, in the form of another boy with MD, was sent the Wagners' way. The boy told Gregory and his mother about the handicapped friendly campus of Edinboro

University. The college, located some 20 miles south of Erie, Pennsylvania, along I-79, is among the nation's standard-setters when it comes to programs designed to help those with a disability.

"We went up for a visit and were really pleased. Everything is wheelchair accessible. They have wheelchair vans to help him get around campus and he'll have a personal care aide to help him get ready each day," Debra explained.

Most importantly for Gregory, the school has a computer science curriculum.

"I'm really excited to go to college, but a little scared, too," Gregory said. "I've never slept alone somewhere before."

While he was busy making his college preparations, the Western New York Chapter of the Muscular Dystrophy Association honored Gregory. He was named the recipient of the 2004 Personal Achievement Award. The honor is rarely given to someone as young as Gregory. It is a testimony to his internal fortitude and to the positive impact that he's had on others suffering from Muscular Dystrophy.

"I was surprised when I found out (that he'd been chosen for the award). It's something that I'm very proud of," Gregory said.

Gregory wrote a paper for a school assignment that detailed his fight against MD. His words speak volumes about the delicate soul residing inside a body at war with itself.

In a chapter entitled "If They Only Knew," Gregory says,

If people only knew how I feel being in a wheelchair, it isn't always fun. Some people say they wish they had an electric wheelchair to ride in all the time. I wish I never had to use a wheelchair because something I want to do is not always accessible. I would rather walk or run to places and do everything I can't do now. Sometimes it's hard to go on thinking about things I used to do, and I always wish I wasn't born with Muscular Dystrophy. I want to be independent, not dependent on people having to help, but everyone, I think, wishes for that. Everyday I hope will be the day when there is a cure and I will be able to do all the things I once could again.
Here is what he wrote in a chapter entitled "A Tough Situation."

I continue to hope for a cure and to be able to jump out of my chair and run all over the place. My life is going to be hard, but I think I can do it. I'll never give up till the very end and you shouldn't either.

"My brother and I used to talk all the time about what we were going to do when we grew up. He loved animals more than just about anything. We were going to go to Seattle and I was going to work at Nintendo and design games and he was going to be the zookeeper at the zoo. I guess it's just up to me now," Gregory confided.

By the time this book arrives at bookstores from its first printing, Gregory Wagner will be a freshman at Edinboro University pursuing his dream of becoming a computer programmer.

It wouldn't surprise me one bit to see a day come in the not-too-distant future when kids all over America are playing video games that have the tagline "Designed by Gregory Wagner" on the back of the box.

Gregory Wagner powers forward in life, pursuing his own dreams, while keeping alive the memory of those of his lost brother.

He'll never give up till the very end and you shouldn't either.

*To learn more about the MDA of WNY, contact:*
*MDA of WNY, 5500 Main Street, #343, Buffalo, NY 14221, Phone: (716) 626- 0035,*
*E-mail: buffalodistrict@mdausa.org*

# Former Professional Ice Skater Empowers Kids By Teaching Them To Skate

*I can do it! I can skate!*
–SABAH Motto

Ironically, it all began with a blindfold.

As America proudly celebrated its bicentennial in 1976, former professional ice skater Elizabeth M. O'Donnell found herself consumed with a notion that, brought to fruition, would see her hailed as one of her country's true pioneers.

Having taught over 25,000 "normal" people to ice skate, would it be possible, Elizabeth dared dream, to teach a blind person to do the same?

To test the theory, she donned a blindfold and put herself through one of her routines. Void of the ability to see, Elizabeth found that she had to trust her other senses more, but that it was indeed possible to skate without sight.

Elizabeth contacted a local school and they sent over her first six blind students.

"I began by putting the skates in their laps. I let them feel the blade. I told them that you are going to put these on your feet and glide across the ice," Elizabeth explained. "I got them down on their hands and knees on the ice and let them feel it. I let them feel the boards around the rink. I also developed a system of guide ropes across the ice so that people wouldn't crash into the boards. Safety has always been a top concern."

Just as Elizabeth had envisioned they would, the students first began to believe in the fact that they could skate, and then actually started doing it. It is imperative to realize that in the late 1970s there were very few, if any, organized sports programs for people with disabilities.

"Things at that time were all exclusive, not inclusive," Elizabeth said. "If a kid had, say, Down's Syndrome, they thought he should only be in programs with other Down's Syndrome kids. I saw a bigger picture."

Part of the bigger picture that Elizabeth saw was that her program need not be confined to kids with visual impairments. Soon, she offered the opportunity to learn to ice skate to all persons with disabilities.

In 1977, taking the sound advice of what she calls one of the programs "angels," Elizabeth formed the Skating Association For The Blind and Handicapped, Inc. (SABAH). With the exception of volunteers she recruited, the not-for-profit educational corporation was, for the better part of 10 years, a one-woman show.

Elizabeth's passionate work for SABAH was fitted around her full-time duties as a skating instructor. She taught figure skating, hockey skating and beginning skating to kids and adults from all around Western New York. The phrase "24-7" is often overused in today's vernacular, but it would have been an apt description of Elizabeth's tireless work in those early days of SABAH.

Lining up volunteers, getting rink owners to provide complimentary ice time, and convincing sporting goods stores to donate equipment, were all things that consumed Elizabeth's time and resources. She did them anyway.

*(Courtesy of K.C. Kratt)*

***Elizabeth O'Donnell.***

In 1979, her hard work culminated in the first of what has become an annual SABAH staple, a feature ice show at Memorial Auditorium (switching to HSBC Arena when the Aud closed in 1996).

"I sent a letter to Joe Figliola, he later became a judge, but was then the Director of Memorial Auditorium. To my surprise, he said, 'Yes'," Elizabeth said. (Years later, Figliola's granddaughter would become one of SABAH's skating stars.)

A crowd of 800 people attended the show, entitled "Boost Buffalo," and saw fifty SABAH stars take center stage in the venerable downtown arena. There was not a dry eye in the house as the kids got to demonstrate the core tenet of the SABAH philosophy for the first time on a public stage. Each boy and girl showed all in attendance: I can do it! I can skate!

Like any great masterpiece, SABAH was painted one brush stroke at a time. The first donated office space came in 1981. By 1985, five separate rinks were playing host to SABAH skaters. In 1986, the SABAH staff increased 100%, to two, as a full-time assistant was hired to aid Elizabeth in the operation of the program. In 1988, 8,000+ people turned out for the 10th Anniversary ice show. In 1990, former president George H. Bush awarded SABAH with the 133rd Point of Light Award. By the end of 1993, the staff size had again doubled to four, with over 1,200 volunteers working with SABAH skaters.

In 1994, Elizabeth designed and tested the very first adaptive skates. In 1997, the first National Chapter of SABAH was opened in Glens Falls, New York. In 2000, the first

SABAH "Home of Miracles" Telethon was held. In 2003, the ice show had over 10,000 attendees. They gave the skaters a seven-minute standing ovation after each performance.

Over the past quarter century, SABAH and Elizabeth have been featured by a host of national media organizations. ABC, NBC, CBS, HBO, TBS, ESPN, Nickelodeon, "Time" Magazine and "Family Circle" are just some of the ones that have sung SABAH's praises. Elizabeth and SABAH have been bestowed with enough awards and accolades to fill a wing of the Smithsonian.

*(Courtesy of K.C. Kratt)*

**Elizabeth with young skater.**

National personalities like Richard Simmons and Spencer Christian have been a part of SABAH's ice shoes, as have skating champions such as Brian Boitano.

Today, over 1,000 skaters participate weekly in SABAH's programs. Nearly 14,000 stars and over 20,000 volunteers have been a part of SABAH since its inception. There are four national chapters of SABAH, with a fifth soon to be added.

When Elizabeth is asked if there is a specific story of a SABAH success that she'd like to share, she, in her typical fashion, refuses the limitations offered in the query.

"There's so many, really. I can remember so many kids who have gone on to college and wrote to keep in touch. I remember the families where volunteers joined to help a sibling. Because of the confidence and belief in themselves that the program nurtured and expanded, there is no way to narrow it down to just one."

Elizabeth is asked what percentage of kids that come to SABAH actually learn to skate?

"We don't measure it like that," she says.

Her description of how SABAH does measure success tells you all you need to know about the depth of love dwelling inside this beacon for Buffalo children.

"Are they having fun? Are they getting healthier? Are they happy? Are they socializing better with people? Is the autistic child looking people in the eyes when they talk to him? Is the kid who always screams in a large crowd, now enjoying being at the mall? Are we making any of our skaters better equipped to have a better quality of life? This is how we measure success."

By teaching kids to skate, Elizabeth is empowering them with the ability to overcome even the most daunting obstacles that stand before them. Elizabeth speaks with great passion and focus. There is one subject, however, that gets the better of her and causes tears to well in her eyes. It is when she speaks of the 50+ kids who came to their first SABAH session on crutches or in wheelchairs, and now have learned to walk independently.

As for the future, Elizabeth can see a day when there will be chapters of SABAH all across America, helping kids gain confidence through skating.

In the time that you've invested in reading this story, it is highly likely that another child has found the courage to step onto the ice and been amazed to find that twenty feet have disappeared under the blades of his or her skates. Another SABAH star has been empowered by those magical words, I can do it! I can skate!

Miracles will continue to happen, all because one woman refuses to remove her blindfold and acknowledge even one reason why they're just not possible.

Author's note: In a letter dated July 13, 2004, SABAH Board Chairman William P. Keefer informed O'Donnell that her employment with the organization would be terminated unless a settlement agreement could be reached.

*(Courtesy of K.C. Kratt)*

*Elizabeth teaching pupil to skate.*

Keefer refused to offer a reason for the decision.

O'Donnell still retains her title as president of SABAH National. She has publicly vowed to continue her efforts to teach blind and handicapped children to ice skate.

*To learn more about SABAH contact:*
*www.Sabahnational.org*

# *It's 11 O'clock – Do You Know Where Your CatchPhrase Came From?*

*It's 11 o'clock. Do you know where your children are?*
–Longtime intro to WKBW-TV Eyewitness News

**W**ant to lose a $20 bet? Walk up to any Western New Yorker over the age of 12 and bet her that she can't finish the following phrase: "It's 11 o'clock – "

If I had made that bet, I'd need a vault full of paper money bearing the likeness of Andrew Jackson, because most of you would instantly reply, "Do you know where your children are?"

It's a phrase that's been part of Western New York vernacular since the late 1960s. Hear it, and visions of retired Channel 7 anchorman Irv Weinstein spring to mind, while the bass-heavy Eyewitness News theme pounds your eardrums.

*(Courtesy of Sean O'Connor)*
**Anne O'Connor.**

What you probably don't know is where the phrase originated. Well, pull up a chair and sit for a spell because, in the famous words of Paul Harvey, I'm about to tell you the "rest of the story."

In the summer of 1967, known as the "summer of love" across America as young men grew their hair long while tripping out to the sounds of the Beatles' "Sgt. Pepper's Lonely Hearts Club Band," Anne O'Connor of Niagara Falls was vacationing in Cape Cod with husband Lloyd and the couple's five boys.

"We always stayed at Holiday Inns," Anne's son, Niagara County Legislator Sean O'Connor said. "We were playing around the pool and Mom overheard one woman asking another if she knew where her children were."

On the long car ride home, Anne, a registered nurse, thought that it might be a good idea in this world of rapidly changing lifestyles for all parents to ask themselves if they knew of their children's whereabouts. Anne's husband Lloyd, a steamfitter and holder of the same county legislator seat that his son Sean would occupy years later, encouraged her to try and take her message to a wider audience.

After kicking around a few ideas, Anne settled on sending the phrase to ABC affiliate WKBW-TV in Buffalo.

On September 18, 1967, Anne received a letter from then Channel 7 News Program Director O. Lyle Koch. For some time, we had been considering an idea similar to yours and felt that your suggestion was excellent. We have, in fact, incorporated your idea into our programming. The first announcement ran on Friday, September 15 and will continue to be broadcast on Monday through Friday at 11P.M.

"There was great anticipation leading up to the first airing," Sean's brother Danny explained. "We were very excited and told all of our friends. It was quite a thrill to have a phrase from inside our family become such a success story."

Sean showed me a note that Irv Weinstein sent his mother in 1982. In it, Weinstein wrote:

"For 15 years we've been wracking our brains trying to remember who gave us that great idea for the 11 o'clock announcement! Thank you...thank you...thank you. Incidentally, your idea has drawn more positive comment from our audience than almost anything we've done."

From that first airing in 1967 until 2003, the phrase was a regular staple of the Western New York TV landscape. There was a period of about two years in the late 1980s when the phrase was removed from the broadcast. Numerous letters and phone calls asking for its return led program officials to bring it back to great fanfare. In 2003, the entire "Eyewitness News" format, along with the "Do you know..." question, was scrapped in an attempt to revive sagging ratings. Most locals feel that the move was ill advised and that it's just a matter of time before the familiar format returns.

Mr. Weinstein now makes his home in Irvine, California. The team of Irv, Sports Director Rick Azar and Weatherman Tom Jolls formed the longest running TV news anchor team in American television history. Irv had this to say about the phrase with which he's so closely associated.

*(Courtesy of Buffalo News, photo by Bill Dyviniak)*
**Irv Weinstein makes a call for the United Jewish Fund in 1989.**

"There is no doubt that it's the signature phrase associated with 'Eyewitness News.' The words contributed to the feeling in the audience that we were more than just distant, cool broadcasters. We were people who cared because we were a part of the community."

Mr. Weinstein explained that there was just one period when the phrase took on an unfortunate connotation.

"99.99% of the comments we received (concerning the phrase) were positive. During the Vietnam War, there were countless Western New Yorkers who were involved in the conflict. Occasionally, we'd get a call or letter saying, 'I'd give anything to know where my son or daughter in the military is right now.'"

A funny sidelight to the phrase is that many Western New Yorkers mistakenly credit Weinstein as the person who recorded the voiceover that opened the "Eyewitness News" broadcast for all of those years.

"I guess because my face was usually the first thing that they saw after the words were spoken, most people attributed the voiceover to me. It was actually recorded by Tom Jolls. It's his voice that was heard," Irv explained.

Because one Niagara Falls woman cared about the children of her community and one broadcasting team cared enough to listen, generations of parents received an important reminder each night before retiring to bed.

Program directors and news formats may come and go, but a seed planted in 1967 has forever changed how Western New Yorkers view the beginning of the 24th hour of each day.

"It's 11 o'clock. Do you know where your children are?"

# Birth of Baby Helps With Healing Process Over 9/11 Attack

*My lovely living boy,  My Hope, my hap, my Love, my life, my joy.*
–Du Bartas – Divine Weekes and Workes.  Second Week, Fourth Day. Bk. II.

*Note: This column was penned on Thursday, September 13, 2001. It first appeared in the September 18, 2001 edition of the Niagara Falls Reporter and was shared by thousands worldwide, via the Internet.*

Two days, two outlooks.

On Tuesday, September 11, I joined the rest of America in officially packaging up our false sense of national security and mailing it back to the black-and-white, Ozzie and Harriet world from which it was unjustly spawned. There can be no doubt that from the moment, at 8:45 A.M., when American Airlines Flight 11 slammed into the north tower of the World Trade Center, the future course of America was permanently altered.

Throughout the 20th century the fight was always "over there." From the two World Wars, through Korea, Vietnam and Desert Storm, we observed attacks from a safe, detached distance. This time it was a home game and the overflow crowd was sent scurrying from the stadium in a state of shock, fleeing for their lives.

At the time of this writing, President Bush has promised a firm, calculated response, not only to the terrorists responsible for the attacks, but also to the countries that financed or harbored them. By the time that you read this, we very well may have begun a full-scale war against any number of nations. Afghanistan, Iraq and possibly even Pakistan, being among them.

I cannot improve upon the president's description of the prevailing emotion of the American people as one of, "quiet anger." I join the multitudes in believing that this is not the hour for pacifism or turn-the-other-cheek ideology, but one for a quick, devastating response on a scale unmatched in American military history.

As the sun rose on a still smoke-covered, eerily deserted Manhattan skyline on Wednesday morning, the initial shock of the attacks began wearing off and I found myself becoming increasingly angered. You see, my wife was nine months pregnant and due at any moment. Bob Dylan's words from the 1960s classic, "Masters of War," were pounding in my head.

You go threatening my babies, unborn and unnamed.
You ain't worth the blood that runs through your veins.

Like an unwatched pot, my rage continued to fester and boil, reaching unprecedented heights. At 3:30 P.M. Wednesday afternoon, I met my wife at her pre-scheduled doctor's appointment.

"My blood pressure's high, they're sending me to the hospital," she told me, tears spilling from her eyes in a sudden torrent.

"We'll probably induce her. She'll be admitted," said Dr. Judith Ortman-Nabi, her OB/GYN.

Suddenly, my perspective shifted. My consciousness was forced from the nation's heartbeat to that of the tiny one beating inside my wife's tummy.

Despite the inducement drugs administered by the nurses at the hospital, my wife's labor progression was nearly nonexistent. The Thursday morning hours blended into the afternoon with little movement in the dilation of her cervix. Continuous network television coverage of the aftermath of the attacks served as a surreal backdrop to our labor room drama. Each hour brought new,

*(Courtesy of Dawn Croisdale)*

**Ryan Jacob Croisdale.**

disheartening statistics. 4,370 people declared missing. 94 already confirmed dead. Adjacent buildings to the World Trade Center on the verge of collapse. 20,000 body bags ordered. Many times I cried as the screen flickered with images of family members desperately seeking loved ones, presumably buried under the tons of concrete, metal and soot.

At 4 P.M. the doctors broke my wife's water. An hour later, there still was no further dilation. Finally, at 5:15 P.M. the decision was made to perform a cesarean section. At 6:11 P.M. on Thursday, September 13, 2001, Ryan Jacob Croisdale, all 6 pounds, 11 ounces of him, was born into the world. Only a little over 57 hours had passed since the first jumbo jet had flown into the World Trade Center tower.

As I held him for the first time, I contemplated the uncertainty of the world which his mother and I had brought him into. A world that had just seen thousands of people senselessly murdered by unfeeling assassins cloaked in the shadows. It is also a world, however, that saw hundreds of brave police and fire personnel sacrifice their own lives to try to save others trapped in the burning towers. It is a world that most likely saw a group of passengers on United Flight 93, from Newark, overpower hijackers and crash the airplane into an abandoned field in Western Pennsylvania. Most likely, they saved thousands of lives at the White House. It is a world that saw people from around the nation stand in line for hours to give blood to aid the Red Cross. And, most importantly, it is a world that saw billions of its citizens speak up, in town squares and prayer circles, about their resolve never to let the agents of darkness force the light from their souls.

In my head, Dylan's lyrics were supplanted by those of another 1960s icon, John Lennon.

You may say I'm a dreamer, but I'm not the only one.
I hope someday you'll join us, and the world will live as one.

When all of the retaliatory bombing and carnage is over, the truest response we can offer to this attack on our nation will come at the personal level. Ryan Jacob's mother and I will fight by empowering him with the concepts of compassion and tolerance. We'll teach him of the principles of freedom and democracy that this great country was founded upon. We'll make sure that he fully understands the storied history of the millions of brave men and women that have died in countless wars defending certain truths that we proudly hold to be self-evident. Among them, life, liberty and the pursuit of happiness.

We'll also make sure that his spirit echoes those of the thousands of rescue volunteers that have bravely given of themselves to save their fellow Americans.

We'll do these things, and many more, to help ensure that the world that our son will one day introduce his own children into will be a kinder, gentler and safer one than he met today.

# *Niagara Falls Woman Sends Love To Daughter In The Form Of A Blooming Garden*

*All this, and Heaven too!*
–Philip Henry

One of the most beautiful things about Western New York is its four distinct seasons.

Autumn brings a cornucopia of colors to greet the great harvest. Tart McIntosh apples offer contrast to the sweet ears of silver corn. Moderate temperatures provide respite from the not-yet-forgotten sweltering days of summer, while the smell of newly fallen leaves offers aromatherapy for the masses.

Winter brings a form of rebirth to our tired, aging cities by providing a blanket of white snow to act like a coat of new paint on a yellowed wall. The rhythmic crunch of it under a boot heel serves to put a spring in our step. Our breath hanging in the crisp air swirls like strokes drawn from the brush of a master painter.

*(Courtesy of Pam Lengen)*

**Helen and George.**

Spring sees the return of robins to our lawn, and daffodils to our gardens. White snow yields to green fields as ponds and creeks return to liquid form. Each year, golfers begin anew their elusive pursuit of a tiny dimpled ball.

Summer provides ninety days of heaven on earth. Neither too hot, nor too cool, the temperature of a Western New York summer is like that of Baby Bear's porridge – just right. From Little League baseball 4th of July fireworks, the days and nights of summer are filled with our greatest resource, the laughter of children.

The story that follows illustrates that there are indeed miracles to be found within these seasons and that sometimes our minds are most awake when we are sound asleep.

Helen and Flo grew up together in the old Polish section of Niagara Falls that surrounded Niagara Street on the East side. In the 1940s, that part of the city was like a little slice of Gdansk right here in the Niagara Frontier. The smell of Polish delicacies like pierogies, borscht and potato pancakes wafted each evening at suppertime from the screen windows. The working-class neighborhood was built in the shadows of the factories that employed so many who had relocated to Niagara Falls in the early days of the Industrial Revolution. Accordion-rich Polka music filled the air, as young girls chased the boys of their fancy with a wisp of pussy willow to celebrate Dingus Day.

Sunday mornings saw St. Stanislaus Kostka Roman Catholic Church filled to the brim with reverent worshippers.

America was filled with hope for the future, and the little Polish neighborhood in Niagara Falls was no exception. It was a time when men were men, women were ladies, and a good friend was a friend for life.

It was no real surprise, then, that the two girls remained friends throughout their lifetimes. They built homes near one another on Saunders Settlement Road in the Town of Lewiston.

While her husband, George, loved to plant and tend to a vegetable garden each year, Helen's passion ran to the nurturing of flowers. A Persian carpet of tulips, daffodils, irises and a wide array of blooming perennials surrounded her home. Helen found a type of peace with her flowers. They offered her, in their communion, a connection with nature that brought her closer to God.

*(Courtesy of Pam Lengen)*

*Helen's garden.*

In George and Helen's later years, her daughter Pam and son-in-law Earle moved upstairs in the two-family home. Earle and Pam continued to tend to her flowers.

In the fall of 2002, George passed away. As it happens for so many couples that share a lifelong bond of love, Helen soon followed him, passing away on January 3, 2003.

As one can well imagine, losing both parents in such a short time frame was very hard on Pam. Fortunately, she had Earle to lean on and found her heart lightening two months later, when the first of Helen's flowers burst through the spring soil to say hello to the world.

As spring tulips and daffodils and primroses gave way to summer irises, daisies, cosmos and dahlias, Pam became aware of a stunning occurrence happening all around her home. Helen's flowers had presented themselves fuller, more vibrant and enchanting than ever before. Now, a more cynical person would have put this event off to some rational explanation, like heavy spring rain or a cyclical high in the fertilization of the soil. Pam, never having lost the belief in spiritual magic that Helen had bestowed her with, knew that there was more than just mere science at play. She knew what the blooming garden truly represented. It was Helen's way of saying that she was okay and doing just fine.

"I wish Helen were here to see this," Pam said, sometimes aloud and sometimes in her head, each day as she stepped outside and saw the garden. "I wish she could see just how beautiful her flowers are this year."

After thinking the thought for the hundredth time, Pam received a call from Flo.

"I've just got to tell you about the dream I had last night," Flo told Pam. "Your mother was waving for me to come over. She took me into the back yard and proudly showed me all her flowers."

What Flo said next took the breath from Pam's lungs and made her knees go weak.

"This looks just like heaven, I said to her," Flo told Pam.

"It is," Helen replied.

In life, there are always seeds that connect the past to the present and one heart to another. Because of a seed of friendship that was planted between two young Polish girls decades ago, a daughter was able to reap the knowledge that her departed mother is safe and happy in a garden that goes by the name of Eden.

# *Local Educator Steams Forward To Preserve History of Underground Railroad*

*How does the Meadow flower its bloom unfold?*
*Because the lovely little flower is free*
*Down to its root, and in that freedom, bold.*
–Wordsworth

"**F**or me, it's all about the quest to keep history alive," Kevin Cottrell said as his deep, soulful eyes seemed to contemplate the heavy weight of the never-ending task that he has assigned to himself.

"With each new generation of children the story must be told anew, so that the great resolve, deeds and sacrifices of so many are not lost to the world."

Kevin sat in a Tim Hortons in the "Little Italy" section of Niagara Falls to discuss a different type of immigrant from the Italians that settled near Pine Avenue in the city's midtown district. He spoke of the proud African men and women that did not elect to come to North America of their own volition, but did choose to escape the bonds of slavery and follow the North Star to freedom across the Canadian border.

Kevin Cottrell is an adjunct professor at the University of Buffalo's African-American Studies Department and is owner/operator of the local tourism and educational company, Motherland Connextions, Inc. The Buffalo native has dedicated his life to telling the story of one of America's greatest inspirational events, the Underground Railroad.

"Don Glynn (columnist for the Niagara Gazette) wrote a piece about the Underground Railroad and I was infatuated by it. I thought, 'Wow, this is really interesting.' At the time (1988), I was working at the Schoellkopf Geological Museum dealing with fauna, slide programs detailing the history of hydropower and of Niagara. I started with Glynn's piece and added a lot of research on my own and put together a slide presentation on the Underground Railroad," Cottrell said.

Cottrell's slide presentation on the Underground Railroad proved immediately popular and soon the Castellani Art Museum asked for his help with a transient art project they were sponsoring that featured sculptures depicting the safe houses of the Underground Railroad.

"That collaboration was so successful, that soon we began to dream of a 15-city tour through the old trail of the Underground Railroad. Mind you, this was all pie-in-the-sky stuff at that time, as we felt like we needed $25,000 to make it happen and we had no money to begin with," Cottrell explained.

Niagara University offered a $1,500 grant and the resourceful Cottrell put the money to good use.

"We converted that money into a T-shirt project called 'Trek a mile in my shoes.' At the 11th hour, we were offered the use of an old church van and we drove to Atlanta, Georgia," Kevin explained.

From Atlanta, the group embarked on an 18-day trek covering 15 cities. Following the Old Harriet Tubman Trail, the group would arrive at each city along the Underground Railroad and speak with the media of their quest and answer questions on the historic significance of the Underground Railroad.

"A news reporter from the Seattle Times picked us up in Philly and rode back with us all the way to Niagara Falls. The Rochester affiliate of PBS picked us up and filmed us from Auburn to St. Catharines, Ontario. They turned the footage into a two-hour documentary called, 'Flight to Freedom,' which was narrated by (Emmy Award-winning actress) Cicely Tyson. When we got to St. Catherine's, we had a big celebration and that event, quite honestly, changed my life forever," Cottrell confided.

"People started calling and asking how much it would be to do the tour that we had done. I had no way to put a price on it, as we'd done it with almost no money in a used van. We were just a group of 9 people, both black and white, who decided to follow a dream. To tell you the truth, it was beautiful. I never cried so many tears of joy in my life. What I did start to think about as I talked to all of these people calling was that, if we could do 18 cities in 15 days, we could surely put together a 5-hour tour and cover the Underground Railroad in Western New York and Southern Ontario."

What began as a group effort soon became a one-man show.

"The people that started the tours with me eventually dropped out, and I just kept going," Kevin said. "Now, some 10 years later, I'm still bringing the story to kids and adults alike."

Cottrell's company, Motherland Connections, provides a myriad of day and extended tours of various points along the Underground Railroad. Cottrell's literature describes the experience of taking a tour with Motherland Connections thusly.
 What better way to understand the Underground Railroad than by following in the footsteps of those brave and hearty souls who took the secret passageways north to Canada. When you experience an Underground Railroad tour with Motherland Connexions, you experience the story of what may be this country's "first multi-cultural humanitarian effort."
Our Underground Railroad Tour means talking about the courage of the Africans who staked their lives for their freedom. It means talking about the many free and enslaved African Americans, Native Americans and European Americans who risked life and property to shelter and sometimes clothe the weary and frightened freedom seekers.

Dressed in period clothing our "conductors" will take you on tours that are more than history lessons - they are life lessons! It's a tool of pride and a better understanding of goodwill. Not just stop and go, our tours are stop and feel - designed to be an emotional and educational experience for both young and old. Embark on a lesson in the triumph of the human spirit. So steal away with us and walk the paths of freedom, courage and love all with the roar of mighty at your feet.

Many of the people experiencing Cottrell's tours are area school kids. Kevin usually finds their minds open to investigating the many inspirational tales connected to the Underground Railroad.

"I usually play the role of the 'Station Master.' I begin the talk in traditional African clothing as I detail what life was like in classical Africa. After I move into the European invasion of Africa, I remove the outer garment and am wearing ragged, slave clothes underneath. The symbolism of the stripping away of African culture and freedom is pretty powerful in helping the kids understand the shock that the initial people sold into slavery experienced," Cottrell explained.

*(Courtesy of Motherland Connextions)*
**Kevin Cottrell.**

Kevin is asked if he's noticed any differences when students of European heritage as compared to Africa-American kids receive his story?

"Oh yeah. A lot of the African-American kids are surprised to learn that so many white abolitionists risked so much to help the slaves. I explain to the white kids that if their families are from the North, then most likely they were abolitionists and never owned any slaves."

Cottrell does get one question – mainly from the younger school children – quite frequently.

"Once they begin to understand what slavery was all about, invariably a hand will shoot up and they'll ask me if I was ever a slave. I just laugh and tell them that the last slave died decades ago. I'm so happy for that question, though, because it shows that we've made a connection. As a preservationist, making connections between the young and history is what it's all about."

Cottrell's tours frequent important points along the Underground Railroad such as the Michigan Street Baptist Church in Buffalo with its hiding rooms and secret passageways, Murphy's Orchard in Burt, New York, where slaves were hidden in an underground room as one of the last stops before crossing into Canada, and a crossing of the lower Niagara River Whirlpool Bridge into Ontario following the same course charted by Harriet "Mother Moses" Tubman.

So important has Cottrell's work been that, in 1998, he was appointed New York State Freedom Trail Commissioner by Governor George Pataki. That same year, Kevin was part of a national coalition that successfully lobbied Congress on the passage of the National Network To Freedom bill headed by the National Park Service, which was signed into law by President Clinton.

Despite all of his accolades, Cottrell is happiest when he's working at the grassroots level and touching the hearts, souls and minds of children of all ages. The children that he educates often take the time to write him in appreciation of the time that they spent learning of the Underground Railroad. Often their simple words speak volumes as to the power of the education process.

When we got on the bus we took off our caps and rode off. The man on the bus talked a lot about slavery. The first place we went to was a red brick church in downtown Buffalo. The man told us that this church had a lot to do about slavery. We talked and had a few laughs but mostly we were just having fun. Also on the field trip we saw Niagara Falls. After a long time on the bus we had lunch. After that we went to a monument that the runaway slaves built. He told us a lot about this monument. Next, we went to the Whirlpool Bridge. He told us a lot about this bridge back in slavery time. When we were walking across the bridge some people were crying and scared. That was an experience that our class will never forget.

Kevin Cottrell looks to the future and envisions an expanded Motherland Connextions that will reach even more people. He will continue to tell the tale of the importance of the Underground Railroad to all citizens of Western New York and Southern Ontario.

Before he finishes the last of his coffee, Kevin is told a story that is prefaced as being both funny and tragic. Last year, a tour of Niagara Falls was arranged for a group of schoolteachers from Long Island. A well-known international firm conducted the tour and it was explained that the guide would be imparting much historical information, including the role of the lower Niagara River as it pertained to the Underground Railroad. The teachers returned from the tour and reported that they had a splendid time, with one glaring exception.

"The guide never spoke one word about the Underground Railroad," one of the teachers said. "So at the end of the tour, we pulled her aside and asked her what she could tell us about it, as it was something that we'd be covering with the kids later in the year. She paused for a good 10 seconds and then said, 'I don't know anything about any Underground Railroad, but I hear that they're going to build a monorail next year.'"

Kevin roared with laughter before taking a moment to reflect on the tour professional's ignorance.

"That right there, in a nutshell, is why my work is not nearly done."

*To learn more about the Underground Railroad, contact:*
*Motherland Connextions Inc., P.O. Box 176 Bridge St. Station, Niagara Falls, NY 14305,*
*Phone: (716) 282-1028*

# Actors And Restored Theater Form A Most Perfect Of Unions

*The novel is more of a whisper, whereas the stage is a shout*
–Robert Holman

It all started with a play called "Wedding Bells." The year was 1923 and a new theater group, the Players of Niagara, had just come on the scene to service the artistic needs of the burgeoning community of Niagara Falls, New York. The troupe was comprised of a bevy of local actors and was headed by an artistic director hired from live theater's hotbed of creativity, New York City.

"The group performed regularly up until December 7, 1941, when the war broke out," said Fran Newton, Executive Director of the Niagara Falls Little Theater. "During the war years, they did some radio theater and things of that sort to stay active. In 1943, they decided to get the group back together and perform a regular schedule of plays. It was then that the name 'Niagara Falls Little Theater' was born."

The first show that the group performed under its new name was titled, "Dr. Ka-Knock." Not exactly Rodgers and Hammerstein, but it was a start. Over the next many decades the group would perform many well-known plays, most of them to standing ovations.

"Beginning in the 1950s and continuing right through to the 1970s, the group was powering straight ahead. Opening nights at the old State Theater on East Falls Street were pulling in nearly 1,000 people. Iney Wallens (a Niagara County radio icon) used to do a red carpet show on live radio at each opening night. She'd interview people on their way into the theater just like they do at the Oscars," Newton explained.

Mrs. Wallens had this to say about those days:

"My husband, Phil, was the director of the board for the Little Theater and I was the musical director. I was a schoolteacher at the time and I contacted Eddie Jo of WHLD-AM and asked him to do a live broadcast with me. He wore a tuxedo and I wore a wedding gown and we handled it just like a Hollywood affair. After we did the first one, he told me that I should have a career in radio and offered me an on-air show. So it was the Little Theater that launched my radio career."

In the 1970s, Shakespearian trained actor Maynard Burgess headed the group. The theater where the troupe performed was named in his honor.

"In 1985, a couple of plays were held at the Greek Theater inside the newly built Niagara Falls International Convention Center. They were huge hits, jam-packed sell-outs, and a decision was made to sell the Maynard Burgess Theater and make a fortune performing at the Convention Center," Newton said.

*(Courtesy of Francis Newton)*

*Frank Cannata performing in "Joseph and the Amazing Technicolor Dreamcoat".*

Unfortunately, the Little Theater trustees had not fully calculated the costs associated with performing at the Greek Theater on a regular basis. Rent, box office expenses and union stagehands added up to more than they had anticipated.  What they found was that unless every show sold out, little money, if any, was made after the books were balanced.

The next decade would see the Little Theater jump around to different venues across the city of Niagara Falls. As a result of some diligent work by a few key people, the theater became financially stable once again.  In 1993, Newton was elected Director of the Theater.

"I was on vacation when they held the meeting where I was nominated, so now the joke is, if you miss a meeting, we're going to put you in charge," said Newton.

During the administration of Niagara Falls Mayor Jim Galie, the Little Theater made a triumphant return to the Greek Theater in the Convention Center.  The vagabond group of actors thought that they had finally found a permanent home. It was a notion that would be driven from their heads by the sound of bells, whistles and clinking coins.

In the summer of 2002, Governor George Pataki, then-Niagara Falls Mayor Irene Elia, and the Seneca Nation announced that the Convention Center would become home to the new Seneca Niagara Casino. The new gaming facility would open for business on New Year's Eve 2002.  Suddenly, the Little Theater would need to find a new home.

"We looked at a number of places around Niagara Falls, none of which worked for one reason or another.  M&T Bank offered us their closed branch on Main Street for free.  We went down and there was a huge vault smack dab in the middle of it. There was nothing we could do with it," Newton explained.

In desperation, the Little Theater attempted to forge a deal with a church on Main Street in the Falls, but that fell through.
Now, it was getting to crunch time.  The group was scheduled to perform "Fiddler on the Roof," late in September 2002.  The management group for the casino gave Fran a verbal commitment that they didn't have to be out of the Convention Center until October 31, enough time to finish the run for "Fiddler on the Roof."

"About late August, as we were rehearsing the play, we started to hear rumors from the maintenance staff that we were going to be asked to leave before the show dates.  I called the mayor and she said that she hadn't heard anything and that we were OK.

Finally, we arrived one day and the maintenance people were cleaning out their lockers. I knew we were in trouble then," Newton said.

On Tuesday, September 18th, just six days before opening night, Newton received a telephone call from then-Niagara Gazette reporter Pat Bradley.

"He said that he'd just spoken to the contractors for the casino and they told him we were out of there immediately. I told him, 'That can't be, I have a verbal commitment from (casino director) Mickey Brown himself.' Pat said that he would reconfirm with his source and called me back later in the day and said, 'They said that there's no way that you're performing in (the Convention Center). It's a hard-hat zone and there's absolutely no way that people will be allowed to come and go inside there for a play.'"

The next day, the Little Theater received a notice, dated September 18th, from the city of Niagara Falls, telling them they had to vacate the Convention Center premises within 24 hours. In other words, here's your hat, what's your hurry?

Newton began frantically calling anyone and everyone he could think of that might have access to a vacant theater. One of the people he contacted was Jim Kretz, Director of the Riviera Theater in North Tonawanda.

The Riviera Theater began very near to the same time that the Little Theater was formed. The Riviera first opened its doors on December 30, 1926, as a state-of-the-art silent film and vaudevillian house. Soon, it went to talkies and drew great crowds not only to watch the movies, but to hear the mighty Wurlitzer Organ play.

Nobody understands the Riviera's history better than Jim Kretz and theater jack-of-all-trades Don Lange.

In 1988, the owner of the theater put it up for sale and it was bid on by Buffalo-born rock funk star Rick James. The man who hit gold with records like "Super Freak" and "Give It To Me Baby" planned to convert the historic theater into a recording studio.

A group of concerned citizens, politicians, and the Niagara Frontier Organ Society put up a counter offer. Their proposal was accepted and the theater rescued. A number of retired carpenters, electricians and plumbers donated their time to restore the theater to the pristine state that it enjoyed in 1926.

Lange loves to give in-depth tours and explain the wonderful work that the retirees did on the historic building.

"We had a sponsorship for the seats. For $30, you could have your name put on a plate on the front of a seat. That money completely paid for their restoration," Lange said.

He also explained how years of smoking in the theater had stained the huge murals that flank either side of the main stage. Due to a masterful restoration process, the murals have regained their natural luster.

The question facing the Niagara Falls Little Theater and the Riviera Theater in the fall of 2002 was, will a partnership between the two entities really work?

*(Courtesy of Riviera Theater)*

***Riviera Theater balcony.***

"We basically had five days from the time we were told that we were out of the Convention Center until opening curtain for Fiddler," Newton explained. "When you've got $13,000 invested into a show and nowhere to perform it, it's a little scary. I called up Jim and said, Let's do it,"

Newton called together every available member of the Little Theater. Together they moved the set, equipment, and as many props and wardrobe as they could handle. Once again, Mickey Brown had given his word that the troupe would have ample time to remove the rest of their possessions.

"On September 26, one day before we opened at the Riviera, someone from the maintenance staff at the Convention Center called and said that they were shutting down the elevator to the Greek Theater the next day and that we had to come get our stuff now," Newton stated. "I called them and told them we are opening a show tomorrow. There's no way we can get anything out now."

Newton was about to receive the jolt of his theatric life.

"One of our members showed up to supervise the move, which the casino had agreed to pay and provide movers for. When she arrived at 8 A.M., she found just about all of our stuff out on the street."
The casino had arranged for a moving team of four men and a 15-foot truck to move 5,000 square feet of equipment and supplies.

"When I arrived on the scene, people (from the community) were going through our costumes. Our entire set for 'Camelot' was in a dumpster," Newton explained.

All in all, most of the Little Theater's possessions were on the street, unattended, for just under four days. Much of what was moved was dirtied, damaged or destroyed.

"I found out later that what they were doing was loading a big cart, taking it up to the second floor of the warehouse we'd rented, and getting up a head of speed before dumping it all on the floor."

Despite the ignoble end to their tenure at the Greek Theater, the Little Theater turned what were most assuredly sour lemons into sweet lemonade. "Fiddler on the Roof" opened to some of the biggest crowds the group had seen since the halcyon days of the 1960s and

1970s. The group turned the dingy warehouse it had rented into a spic and span storage facility, complete with a rehearsal stage. Also, the theater's relationship with the Seneca Niagara Casino weathered the initial storm and today the casino is a major supporter of the theater troupe.

After some initial tension with the Organ Society at the Riviera, the Little Theater now brings in revenue that helps ensure that the mighty Wurlitzer Organ will continue to be heard by young and old alike. Frank Newton, along with two other members of the Little Theater, now sit on the Riviera's Board of Directors.

"It's sad that we had to leave the city limits of Niagara Falls, but much of our current customer base was coming from the Tonawandas already," said Newton. "To survive in the new millennium, we needed to be a regional theater and now we truly are."

A recent event illustrated the point that the Little Theater now has a new audience. A woman entered the Riviera and bought tickets from Jim Kretz to see the Little Theater's production of "The Fantasticks."

*(Courtesy of Riviera Theater)*

**Riviera Theater.**

"It's the longest running play on Broadway, you know," Kretz told the woman.

"Oh, I'd never go to New York," came the reply.

"It played in Buffalo recently, but I think we have a much stronger production," Kretz countered.

"I don't go into Buffalo, either. I've been waiting for it to come here for years and now I'm finally going to get to see it," the woman said, as a smile spread over her face.

Seventy-eight years ago, the ribbon was cut on a beautiful theater in North Tonawanda. Just three years earlier, a theater troupe in Niagara Falls responded to a rousing ovation by bowing gracefully to the audience for "Wedding Bells."

Little did they know then that the wedding bells tolled for the beautiful marriage that the two would one day enter into.

*For more information on the Niagara Falls Little Theatre and the Riviera Theater, contact: The Niagara Falls Little Theatre, Inc., PO Box 160, North Tonawanda, NY 14120, www.nflt.com*

*The Riviera Theater, 67 Webster Street, North Tonawanda, NY, www.rivieratheater.org*

# *Williamsville Couple Circles The Wagons In Support Of Son*

*We make a living by what we get,*
*But we make a life by what we give.*
–Winston Churchill

There may be no more anticipated event in the life of a married couple than the birth of their first child. Dreams of first steps and first words, learning to tie a shoelace and how to ride a bike fill a mom and dad-to-be's heads. Above everything else, an expectant couple prays for a healthy child. "Just let the baby have ten fingers and ten toes and I'll be happy," is a common response to the question, "What do you want, a boy or a girl?"

The story that follows details a Williamsville couple's journey through the difficult birth of their son, Christopher, and the tragic news that followed. One that would see them overcome the heartbreak of learning that their newborn had severe brain damage, to realize the joy they would receive from the love of a very special boy.

When Kenny and Cindy Deubell were expecting their first child fourteen years ago, everything throughout the first nine months of the pregnancy had gone extremely well. When Cindy went into labor and was admitted into the hospital, there was no reason to expect that anything but a normal, healthy birth was in store. Everything was fine up until the latter stages of the labor process, when an emergency Cesarean Section was performed.

"When the C-section was ordered all hell broke loose. I was up by Cindy's head while they did it. We heard Christopher cry once, then he didn't cry anymore," Kenny explained. "I looked at the floor and it was covered with a green liquid that looked like pea soup. They asked me if I wanted to come over and see my son. I went over and looked at him. He still wasn't crying. They said, 'OK, Mr. Deubell, now you have to go.'"

With those words, the dreams the Deubells had of having a healthy newborn were ripped away. Their lives were turned upside down.

"Christopher was put in an incubator and taken to Children's Hospital while Cindy had to stay here," Kenny explained.

For eight days, Christopher was on life support. It was feared that he wouldn't survive. Kenny was thrown into the most surreal of nightmares. His life was transformed from being the proud papa handing out congratulatory cigars, to the grim reality of commuting between two hospitals. One housed his heartbroken wife attempting to recover from major surgery and the other contained his newborn son clinging to life by the narrowest of threads.

"A nurse came after they'd taken Christopher to Children's and told me that there was a chance that he might not make it through the night," Cindy recalled. "I called down to the switchboard and said that I didn't want any calls coming through unless it was my mom and dad or Kenny. Usually, when you have your first child, you get calls of congratulations, flowers and hugs. I was devastated that none of those things were going to happen, and that I was separated from my little boy."

After four days had passed, Cindy was finally cleared to be released from the hospital and Kenny took her to Children's to see Christopher. More than 100 hours after she'd given birth to him, Cindy Deubell held her son for the first time.

"They put Christopher into my arms and all I remember is uncontrollably crying. I don't think I've ever cried that hard in my life, to this day," Cindy explained.

*(Courtesy of Deubells)*

**Cindy, Christopher and Kenny Deubell.**

Doctors told the Deubells that Christopher had suffered extensive brain damage and that it would retard the development of all of his motor skills and functions. Some of the initial doctors that saw Christopher were lacking in the skills needed to provide good bedside manner.

On one visit back to the hospital, when Christopher was about 6-months-old, a doctor said something to Kenny that he will never forget.

"(The doctor) came in and clapped his hands twice over Christopher, then he said to me, 'Mr. Deubell, have you and your wife thought about having another child?' I said, 'No, we haven't thought about anything but Christopher.' He said, 'Well, I think you should, because your son is going to be a vegetable.' Quote, unquote."

Faced with such non-supportive medical guidance and little Christopher's daily struggles, it would have been easy for the Deubells to give in completely. They could have easily written off Christopher's life as his doctors were doing. But Kenny and Cindy are fighters and decided to take matters into their own hands.

"We kept a yellow legal pad and detailed every aspect of Christopher's care on it," Kenny said. "The time, date and severity of the seizures he was having, the time, amount and type of medications they were giving him, the whole nine yards. When a doctor would come in and put up a graph and say that Christopher had 95% brain damage, I'd say, 'OK, but what are we going to do to help him?'"

Eventually, Christopher's case was taken over by Dr. Patricia Duffner, one of the top neurologists in America, whom he still sees today. The Deubells set their minds on helping Christopher achieve all that he could in life. As a result, he has far exceeded the expectations for someone with his severity of brain damage and cerebral palsy (which he was subsequently diagnosed with, as a result of the brain damage he suffered during birth).

Today, the brown-haired, blue-eyed, boy attends classes at The Cantalician Center. Despite the fact that he's not supposed to be able to talk, he constantly melts his mother's heart by uttering the word "mama." Christopher loves bath time. A ride on the lift that helps him in and out of the bathtub always brings a smile to his face. And Christopher loves to spend time in the whirlpool with his dad. Christopher has traveling in his blood, as he loves to go cruising in the Deubells' van. More than all of that though, Christopher loves music. A Shania Twain album is his favorite. What else would you expect from a 14-year-old red-blooded boy?

Recently, the Deubells received a real treat when their niece, Shannon, made Christopher the subject of an assigned school essay on the subject of a special person.

Shannon began her essay:

I have a very special cousin named Christopher. He is special because he has a disability called Cerebral Palsy, which he was diagnosed with at birth.

She closed the essay with these words:

Also, Christopher is a very cute 14-year-old boy with brown hair and very bright blue eyes. He is about 4 feet, 10 inches tall. I love my cousin, Christopher, very much, even if he does have a disability.

When you see all three of the Deubells together, the love that flows between them is quite apparent. Christopher has already outlived his life expectancy and, with the love of his parents fortifying him, has a bright future ahead.

Kenny and Cindy are asked if they could ever imagine their lives without Christopher?

"No," they answered in unison.

Kenny then said something that he probably never would have imagined possible on the day of Christopher's birth.

"A life without Christopher just as he is wouldn't be a life worth living."

# *Bills Fans Support Family In Their Hour Of Need*

*Who can foretell for what high cause*
*This darling of the Gods was born?*
–Andrew Marvell

It's called a "bump."

In Internet message board parlance, to "bump" a message or "thread" is to add a new reply to the original posting, thereby "bumping" it back to the top of the listing. Without a bump, messages fall back in the listing order, and then disappear altogether. On December 9, 2002, the Gioia family of Seattle, Washington, rode the first waves of quite possibly the greatest Internet bump of all time.

Paul Gioia was born just yards from the Peace Bridge, which connects Buffalo, New York, with Fort Erie, Ontario. His family soon moved to the Eggert Road section of the Queen City. The Gioias quickly fell in love with the blue-collar neighborhood built by the sweat and toil of a cross-section of European immigrants who were proud to set down firm roots in the new land of America. It was while living there that Paul learned of the resiliency of the people of Western New York. Economic downturns, blizzards and condemning national press have all served to build a backbone in the denizens of Buffalo that can never be broken.

Years later, it would be that unbending community backbone that would help hold up Paul and his family in their greatest hour of need.

After high school, Paul spent many years in New York City before moving west to Seattle for a job opportunity. There, he met a young lady from Houston, Texas, named Angela and the two hit it off and began to date. Somehow, this mix of East Coast moxie and refined Southern charm struck a perfect chord within each of them and the two were married.

As Kurt Cobain was using "Grunge" music to make Seattle the hippest city in America, an old yearning began to visit Paul in the quiet hours of his mind. It was a call back to the days of his youth in Buffalo.

"I was never much of a Bills fan as a kid," Paul said by telephone from his Seattle home. "I just remember my grandfather and his friends loving to watch O.J. run with the football."

As a way to find a connection back to his city of birth, Paul became a passionate fan of the Buffalo Bills. He got DirecTV to watch all of the games and surfed the Internet to find any information he could on the red, white and blue Bills.

"You just don't find people in Seattle that are like the people of Buffalo," Paul said. "That internal fortitude, maybe it's because of the snow and cold winters, even the four Super Bowl losses, the people just refuse to say die or ever give in. I knew that I needed to get connected back to that way of thinking."

Paul became a regular visitor to a Web site that catered to fans of the Bills. After that address was suspended, Paul stumbled upon Two Bills Drive, the Web site that would one day make an impact on his life that he will never forget.

A popular section of Two Bills Drive is a message board called The Stadium Wall (TSW). There, Bills fans talk about the team 365 days per year. New coach hires, free agent signings, game analysis and spirited debate as to whether Mighty Taco or the Garbage Plate is Western New York's best indigenous food, it's all discussed in it's finest minutia at TSW.

Paul became a regular contributor at TSW, posting under the screen name Thirdborn, and in the spring of 2002, he used the board to make the announcement that he and Angela were expecting their first child together in December. The pregnancy progressed normally and Paul and Angela found themselves excited about bringing another fan of the Buffalo Bills into the world.

On Friday, December 6, 2002, Angela was in a Seattle hospital in labor with what turned out to be a baby boy – August Salvatore Gioia. All seemed to be going well until things took a tragic turn for the worse just before the baby was born.

On the evening of December 9, 2002, an exhausted Paul took a brief respite from the hospital bed of Angela, where he had spent almost all of the proceeding 72 hours, and posted this message on TSW:

My wife went into labor Friday night, and the baby's cord collapsed leaving him without oxygen for too long. After a brutal emergency caesarian, my son wasn't breathing, and had no heartbeat. It took ten minutes to bring him back, and I've been told that there's a 90% chance that he has suffered severe brain damage. My wife is fine, and my son is off the ventilator. We won't know anything more for days and I won't be posting anytime soon. He's strong, but we all need your prayers. His name is August Salvatore Gioia. Thanks!
"I ride with the boy King."

Gus, as his family would come to call him, was diagnosed with Hypoxic Ischemic Encephalopathy (HIE), sometimes known as neonatal encephalopathy. HIE is an acquired syndrome characterized by evidence of acute brain injury due to asphyxia. The doctor on staff the night of Gus' birth erroneously told Paul that his son had little chance of surviving more than a week (in truth, the mortality rate for severe cases of HIE is roughly 50%) and that if he did, he had little hope for a life beyond a vegetative state.

As you can imagine, this news hit Paul like a ton of bricks. With Angela still heavily sedated, Paul had to make some very difficult decisions concerning Gus' treatment on his own.

Paul put out a call of distress to his family and soon the cavalry was on its way. Two of Paul's brothers drove non-stop from their out-of-town residences to be at his side.

*(Courtesy of Paul Gioia)*

**Gus in his Bills uniform.**

As Paul looked into the eyes of his beautiful little baby boy, he saw something there that was eerily familiar. It was a look of determination. It was the same look that he'd seen in the eyes of those who struggled through the Blizzard of '77. It was a look that he'd seen many times on the faces of his gridiron heroes, the Buffalo Bills. It was that exact look that took the team to four consecutive Super Bowls, a feat unmatched in the annals of the National Football League. It was that look that carried the team back from a 32-point deficit to defeat the Houston Oilers in a 1992 wildcard playoff game, better known as the greatest comeback in NFL history. And it was precisely that look that inspired ESPN host Chris Berman to coin the phrase, "Nobody circles the wagons like the Buffalo Bills."

It was while thinking about these things that one of Paul's brothers spoke just the words that he needed to hear.

"He said that no matter what, we can do it," Paul explained. "The Gioia family isn't going to give up."

The second shot of tonic that Paul needed came when he checked in at TSW a few days later.

"I really didn't expect a groundswell. When I saw what was happening, it just floored me," Paul said.

What he found was the thread to his original message about Gus' complications during delivery filled with hundreds of posts. Each of them pledged prayers for angels to look after Gus.

Here are a few of those posts:

*These words may sound trite and it's impossible to convey true thoughts over this impersonal medium, but rest assured that your friends here (and even the gang at the PPP board) have you and your family in our hearts. – GG*

*I will pray all day and ask my family to do the same.*
*Please keep us posted, and feel the support you have.*
*May God bless you and your family. – Bill from NYC*

*I can't tell you how this bothers me. My prayers are with you. – Ice*

*I am meeting with Drew (Bledsoe) and his Dad at a Church tomorrow--and you can count on their prayers too. They have 3 little boys of their own. And remember, kids are tough little suckers and doctors, although educated, are frequently wrong.*
*God bless. – Ann Infamous*

"These people, most of whom don't even know me and my family, got me through that first week," Paul said. "One guy even took a picture of Gus to his work and had the people there pray for him. What they did was amazing."

On December 10, 2003, at precisely 6:37 P.M., Cablelady made the first of hundreds of postings with the same one-word message that would be added to the thread – Bump!

For nearly seven months, the thread was kept alive by posters who wouldn't let Gus out of their hearts for even one moment. As the weeks and months passed, Gus went home and made steady progress. As Paul would add updates to the thread, the good news that he posted was always met with smiles and tears of joy on TSW.

Sometimes posters would log on to wish Gus a Merry Christmas or a Happy Easter, while other times it was simply to say goodnight and God bless.

There is no doubt that the thread would never have died out of its own volition. Worried that it was taking up so much bandwidth that it was in danger of crashing the TBD site altogether, Paul contacted the site administrator, Scott, and asked that the thread be retired.

Scott had no concerns over the size of the thread, but as he was in the process of changing message board software anyway, all posts from the old database were unable to be imported. Scott archived the thread and all 952 posts of it can forever be viewed at: http://www.twobillsdrive.com/gus/.

Scott has this to say about the response by Two Bills Drive members to Paul's posting: "The love and compassion that we have for one another defines us as a community. The outpouring of prayers may have surprised Paul and his family, but it was not a surprise to me. Time and again, this community closes ranks around its members to provide emotional support when needed. Paul, Angela, and Gus will always hold a special place in the hearts of their extended family on the Stadium Wall."
Other threads to Gus are constantly being created and he will always be a permanent part of life at TSW.

Today Gus is continuing to make steady progress. He has begun to vocalize, is making strong eye contact, and Paul and Angela are teaching him sign language. He is seen by some of the nation's premier neurologists at Children's Hospital of Seattle and receives regular physical therapy and early intervention sessions.

Gus is a Gioia and he is a survivor.

Paul has a goal of one day bringing Gus back to Buffalo for a Bills game and to meet with the people that have touched their lives by offering their prayers on TSW.

When that day arrives, you can be sure that Gus will be surrounded by the beating hearts of hundreds of people, united by their love of a team and a city that never says die, who form a safety net that will always be strung up under his high wire. Those hearts will beat in harmony for the boy king of Seattle and it will sound just like this – Bump, Bump, Bump.

# Heroic Firefighter Saves Life Of Man With A Little Help From His Friends

*I have no ambition in this world but one, and that is to be a firefighter...*
*Our proudest endeavor is to save lives of men-the work of God Himself. Under the*
*impulse of such thoughts, the nobility of the occupation thrills us and stimulates us*
*to deeds of daring, even at the supreme sacrifice. Such considerations may not*
*strike the average mind, but they are sufficient to fill to the limit our ambition in life*
*and to make us serve the general purpose of human society.*
–Chief Edward F. Croker FDNY circa 1910

If I were to say the words "on the brink" to you, what images would spring to mind? Usually the phrase is used metaphorically to illustrate extreme states of emotion at polar opposite ends of the human experience. "We're on the brink of success" or "I'm on the brink of disaster."

On March 19, 2003, Niagara Falls Firefighter Gary Carella was put into the unique situation of experiencing the phrase "on the brink" both metaphorically and literally, all at the same time.

"It started at shift change, around 4:30 - 5 o'clock. A call came in concerning a man trapped at the top of the falls," Carella explained from a meeting room at Firehouse 4 on 10th Street in the Cataract City. "Now, 90% of the time, to us, 'trapped at the top of the falls' means somewhere off of Goat Island. It was quite a shock when we arrived to see where he actually was. It was hard to imagine that someone could be that close (to the crest of the Horseshoe Falls) and not go over."

What Carella and his comrades from the fire department saw was a 47-year-old male attired in dress slacks, a shirt, a tie and a windbreaker jacket standing in the thigh-deep water of the upper Niagara River just a few feet before it plunges some 176 feet over the Canadian Horseshoe Falls. The water at that juncture of the river travels at about 20 miles per hour as 700,000 gallons of it, per second, cascades over the 2,200 feet crest of the largest of Niagara's three waterfalls.

"On the way there, I'd gone through the mind scenario that we are taught to utilize for all water rescues. I'm going to need my water ropes, we're going to need the cold water rescue suits. You kind of get all of your thoughts in line before arriving on the scene," Carella said.

When the firefighters arrived at the falls, the New York State Park Police, who had been the first to respond to the man's plight, handed over control of the situation to Battalion Chief John Jacoby.

"Because of the ice and the fencing around Terrapin Point (the scenic overlook of the Horseshoe Falls from the U.S. side of Niagara is fenced off each winter due to dangerous icy conditions caused by Niagara's mist) we were about 350-400 feet from where the guy was trapped. Our biggest problem at that point was getting our equipment to the scene," Carella explained.

Once the captain assessed the situation and gave his orders, Carella and his fellow rescuers sprang into action.

"We took our ropes and gear and used our Stokes basket, which is usually used to carry injured patients in, as a sled to get our gear across the ice. We just came over the crest and for the first time we get to see the proximity of the gentleman to the edge," said Carella.

One has to wonder just what goes through a person's mind at a moment like that.

"We hear the word 'expedite' all the time in this job. Just about every call we go on, we're told to 'expedite.' At that moment that word became very real to me. I began to think, how much longer can he hold on? Do we have enough time to make a successful rescue?" Carella stated. "You start to race your mind at 100 miles per hour, because any second you might waste, might be the last second that the guy has to hold on."

You might think that a person in Carella's spot might become absorbed in worrying about his own safety.

Carella didn't, mainly due to the confidence that he has in the other members of his fire hall.

"One of the first things they teach you is that, as a rescuer, you never want to be in the position of having to be rescued. We had a sound plan, with back-ups, and I knew that I could count on the guys who were with me."

*(Courtesy of Lorry Malkowski)*

**Gary Carella, second from left, with Capt. Kevin Caffery, Officer Litzinger, Sgt. Patrick Moriarty.**

The first plan was to call for a helicopter piloted by Capt. Kevin Caffery and Officer Arthur Litzinger from the Erie County Sheriff's Office to see if they could lower a line down to the man.

"We (State Park Police Sergeant Pat Moriarty and Carella) entered the water with our line and kept a safe distance so that the helicopter could do its job," Carella said. Unfortunately, there was an unforeseen problem that would make the rescue far more dangerous than had even been imagined. The torrent of water that plunges over Niagara Falls creates an energy force that shoots up into the sky above the cataracts. This force played havoc with the stability of the helicopter.

Once the helicopter was stabilized, the pilot had to get very low to the water to attempt to drop a line to the stranded man. This tactic created a new problem. The downward air force from the spinning propeller repeatedly knocked the man over and nearly sent him to his death over the falls.

"At that point we went to Plan B, which was to throw him the rescue buoy. Because of the way that the current was moving, that didn't work either, so we combined the two rescue plans," Carella explained.

By this time, the power authorities on both the U.S. and Canadian sides of Niagara Falls had been notified and the control dams, which regulate water flow over the falls, had been opened. Thus cutting the flow of water to the cascades in half.

Carella and his fellow rescuers believe that the man must have found a fissure in the rock that he was able to use to lock his feet in, otherwise he would have never been able to withstand the current for as long as he did.

As Carella and Moriarty began working their way toward the man, they attempted to keep his spirits up by shouting words of encouragement and giving him the "thumbs up" sign. The mental aspect of a rescue is just as important as the physical part. A victim needs to be an active participant in his or her own rescue. Hope is the key ingredient in the recipe that self-empowers a victim.

As Carella and Moriarty were yelling to him that everything was under control, the stranded man sent them a sign that his will was not broken.

"He looked at his watch and then back at us as if to say, 'What's taking so long?' We knew then that mentally he was still with us," Carella said.

Another concern for the rescuers was the very real threat of hypothermia.

"I was in a permeated suit designed to keep you dry in the water," Carella explained. "When I finally got out (after being in the frigid water for an hour), I was numb to the bone. How he stayed in there for an hour and a half with the type of clothes he had on speaks volumes about the human spirit to survive."

After numerous setbacks, including the man being knocked over twice by the back draft created by the helicopter's rotors, the luck that the rescuers were waiting for finally arrived.

The rescuers on the helicopter had been throwing a ring tethered to a line out to the man. With every attempt, the current from the river washed the ring back. The men were afraid to overthrow the ring for fear that the victim would reach for it and lose his footing or that the line would wrap around and dislodge him, either way sending him over the falls.

"The guys in the helicopter threw the ring out and let the current carry it back toward the guy. The rotor's wash had knocked him over and his feet actually swung out over the falls. He was falling down and he reached out with one hand and caught the ring.

We then began to drag him toward the shore," Carella explained.

The rescuers were in for one last surprise as the man became lodged under the massive ice build-up that is created each winter above Niagara Falls.
"Once we realized that he was caught, Pat (Moriarty) starts yelling, 'Stop!' He then said to me, 'We've got to go in and get him,'" Carella said.

What Gary explained next paints a most dramatic picture of the imminent danger that all of the men found themselves in.

"Pat went out the rope and grabbed the guy by four fingers on one of his hands. They were just four feet from the brink and that hold on four fingers was all that was preventing that guy from certain death."

Carella then swung into action.

"I got up to where they were and was able to get a rescue loop around his arm. Pat then was able to get a better hold and I went under the ice and got what's like a wrestling hold on him, a full body lock. Pat yelled to the guys on the other end of the line to pull and they got us up on the ice."

What had unfolded over an hour and a half was over in seconds. With twenty men pulling on shore, the victim and his heroic rescuers were finally back on firm ground.

Cheers went up all around as medical personal attended to the victim. As a result of his actions, Gary Carella was named New York State Firefighter Of The Year. He became only the second man from Niagara Falls ever so honored.

Gary is quick to acknowledge that it is an award that he accepted on behalf of all of the rescuers that worked so hard to save that man at the brink of the falls.
"Pat Moriarty of the State Parks Police, Captain Kevin Caffery and Officer Artie Litzinger from the Erie County Sheriff's Department and all of the guys from the fire department who held my life in their hands that day, they deserve as much credit as I do," Carella said. "We were successful in giving that man his life back just as it was before he decided to go into the water. I'm just so proud to be associated with this group of men, they're all heroes."

Because of the professionalism of a group of dedicated rescuers, there is a lucky man who finds himself blessed to contemplate a new brink.

The brink of tomorrow.

# *Niagara Falls Man Adopts A New Philosophy That Leads To A Better Life*

*It takes a village to raise a child.*
–Hillary Rodham Clinton

**D**oug Abel believes in the innate goodness of children. Maybe more importantly, he believes that some kids just need one break in their lives to turn things around. Our society is quick to write a bad kid off as incorrigible and beyond the grasp of rehabilitation. Doug is convinced that you'll find pieces of wheat buried within the chaff, ones just begging for a new beginning.

Abel is a rare bird in today's world, he's a single dad who is also a foster parent.

"In 1994, a friend of my son, Nick, showed up at our house at 2 o'clock in the morning bleeding and hurt. He'd been beaten up by his father. It happened a couple more times and then he showed up with a broken arm. We took him to the hospital and ended up keeping him," Doug said. "He stayed with us for about six months and, I was married at the time, I said to my wife, 'Why don't we help some other kids and become foster parents?'"

The Abels contacted the Hillside Children's Center and began the formal process of becoming foster parents.

"There's quite an extensive background check that's done, plus a lot of questionnaires that are filled out along with some intensive interviewing," Doug explained.

The Abels were approved and soon kids were getting a new lease on life by spending time as part of their household.

"When I was married, we were sent a lot of girls," Abel explained. "At least one time we had a full house of girls and that wasn't easy to manage."

Now there are thousands of foster parents in Western New York, most of them doing a commendable job in helping children, but what makes Abel's story special is that he was allowed to continue to be a foster parent after he and his wife divorced.

"I was always the one who did all of the paperwork and met with the people at the agency," Doug told me. "I had established a track record of having very good success with teenaged boys and that's what I specialize in now."

I asked Doug what the process normally consists of when a new boy is placed in his care.

"There's almost always a testing period. Kids test you to see how much they can get away with. Once you set the rules, things usually settle down after the first week," Abel said.

Doug expects the boys to live by a few basic tenets.

"I tell them that they have to do well in school by excelling at their homework. I tell them that they have to take care of themselves physically, including good hygiene, and I tell them that they have to respect the other people in the household."

Not surprisingly, most of the boys react favorably to the structure that Doug provides for them.

"I think that many of these boys crave discipline. The only thing that most of them have known is abuse, they are looking for a male figure who is strict, yet supportive," Doug told me.

Doug explained that most of the kids he houses are with him until they "age out" of the program, usually a time period of about 18 months to three years. One of the most difficult things that Doug must do to bond with the boys is to gain their trust, a trust that has often been destroyed due to years of neglect or abuse.

*(Courtesy of Frank Croisdale)*

***Volunteerism statue, Niagara Falls, New York.***

"It's a given that, in most cases, the home life is not good. Many of these kids have experienced all sorts of abuses and the worst part is that they've suffered them at the hands of the very people that should have loved and protected them," Abel confided.

One such boy who was sent Doug's way ended up making a dramatic impact on the foster dad's life.

"Lucas* was 10 when he was first sent to me. He'd been physically, emotionally and sexually abused by both of his parents. He was in desperate need of a stable situation and someone he could trust, I'm glad that someone was me," Doug said.

Many of the kids in the foster care system see a mental health professional for counseling. Once a child is placed in his care, Doug often attends the sessions to help ease the child's

*Not his real name.

transition into a new home. Doug will never forget the words that Lucas spoke to a counselor when asked the question of why he was in foster care.

"I'm here because I had to put both of my parents in jail."

Lucas' birth parents each received 30-year sentences for his abuse and molestation and won't be eligible for parole for many years.

"When he said that, it just broke my heart," Doug confided. "I knew his background, but just imagine being a child and having to send your parents to jail."

Doug and Lucas became fast friends and Lucas began to thrive in his new surroundings. Doug, a general contractor specializing in carpentry, began to teach Lucas the trade that provided him a good living. Soon Doug began to think that Lucas should become a permanent part of the Abel family.

"I loved him just like one of my own boys and I asked him if he'd like to stay here permanently."

When Lucas answered in the affirmative, Doug began the process of formally adopting the boy. Lucas was 13 when the adoption became legal, he's 15 today. His memory of the abuses he suffered is slowly fading as he builds new memories with a family that loves him.

Doug Abel continues to open his heart and his home to boys in need. He now teaches classes in foster parenting skills to those new to the process. Doug conducts a benefit each year to send foster kids for a fun-filled day at area theme parks like Six Flags or Fantasy Island. For many of the kids, it's the first time they've even been to an amusement park.

As we were concluding our interview, I asked Doug what he would take with him from his foster parenting experiences.

"When the phone rings and it's a kid that you had with you, maybe years ago, who calls and says, 'Here's what's going on at home, what do you think I should do?' Knowing that what they learned in your home was that an adult can be trusted and that they still have that trust in you years later, that's what I'll hang my hat on, right there."

For Lucas, and for the many other kids fortunate enough to spend time living with Doug Abel, the love and guidance of a positive male role model was just what they needed to start over in life. Now they possess something they never did before, they foster hope for a brighter tomorrow.

*To find out more about becoming a foster parent, contact:*
*Hillside Children's Center, 712 Main Street, Buffalo NY 14202, 716 848-6400*

# If You Don't Wise Up, You're Going To Father Baker's

For a certain generation of Western New York kids, they are words that signaled mom and dad meant business. "If you don't wise up, you're going to Father Baker's!"

While most parents used their threat as a tool to encourage good behavior, being sent to Father Baker's school for orphaned and destitute boys was a blessing for thousands of children. Father Nelson Baker spent his life in the humble pursuit of helping his community's poor, hungry and forsaken. In the annals of the history of Western New York, never before or since has one man made such a dramatic impact on so many. A legacy that began in 1854 lives on today as the Our Lady Of Victory Institutions continue to build bridges under those citizens of our community who are struggling to keep their heads above water.

*(Courtesy of Our Lady of Victory Institutions)*
**Father Baker.**

Nelson Baker was born in Buffalo on February 16, 1841, as the son of a grocer. Young Nelson knew Buffalo as a thriving metropolis that benefited greatly due to its prime positioning along the Erie Canal. Nelson's mother, Caroline Donellan, was a devout Irish Catholic and it is roundly believed that it is from her that his deep faith was inherited.

A barely matured Nelson Baker enlisted in the 74th Regiment, New York State Militia, to fight for the North in the Civil War. It was during that period of his life, one where he witnessed injury and death on an almost daily basis, that Nelson Baker first began to entertain notions of becoming a priest.

After the North secured victory, Nelson returned home to Buffalo and entered into business with partner Joseph Meyer. Before the two consummated their deal, Baker confided to Meyer that he was thinking heavily of joining the priesthood. It was while in business with Meyer that Nelson Baker first came in contact with the orphans at the St. Joseph's Boys Home in Lackawanna, then known as Limestone Hill.

"I am convinced in my own heart that his involvement with these kids brought about the fruition of the seeds of a vocation that had already been planted within him. The desire to become a priest and to serve more fully, he received permission to enter the seminary," Msgr. Robert Wurtz said as he sat in his office at OLV along with Marketing Director Beth Donovan.

Baker entered Our Lady Of The Angels Seminary in Niagara Falls in September of 1869. Two years into his studies, Baker contracted erysipelas, known as "St. Anthony's

Fire" during the Middle Ages, a painful skin infection that can cause disfigurement and even death.

"It was in doubt at that time, due to his illness, if he would become a priest, " Msgr. Wurtz explained. "He asked permission to travel to Rome to pray and his request was granted. A stop was made in Paris and it was there that Father Baker first became acquainted with the famous shrine of Our Lady Of Victory and the many miracles that had been reported there. He made a promise that, if he were ordained as a priest, he would devote his entire priesthood to Our Lady Of Victory."

It was a promise that Nelson Baker would fulfill as, on the Feast of St. Joseph in 1876, he was ordained to the priesthood by Bishop Ryan of Buffalo. The newly ordained priest was assigned to St. Patrick's parish in Limestone as an assistant to Father Hines. St. Patrick's oversaw the St. Joseph's Orphanage and the St. John's Protectory - both were heavily in debt. After five years of swimming in the red ink at St. Patrick's, an exhausted Father Baker requested a transfer and was assigned to St. Mary's Parish in Corning, New York.

It has been said that God is meant to know, while man is meant to wonder. Those words would have been of great comfort to Father Baker in 1882 as he was summoned by Bishop Ryan to return to St. Patrick's to take over for Father Hines. Father Baker, remembering the sea of debt at Limestone Hill, initially refused his Bishop's request. When Bishop Ryan insisted, with the words, "Nelson, go out to Limestone Hill and do the best you can. I will pray that God will be with you," Father Baker acquiesced and returned home to Western New York.

The debt problem at St. Patrick's had only grown during Father Baker's absence. Upon arriving, the man of the cloth was accosted by several creditors, each of whom demanded payment in full for outstanding balances. Father Baker pleaded for patience. His pleas fell on deaf ears. Father Baker then did something that would become a theme for the rest of his life; he embraced the power of poverty. The next morning, Father Baker cleaned out his personal savings account and paid off several of the creditors. Not before telling them that by accepting his money they were not only settling their bill, but were also forfeiting the right to do future business with St. Patrick's. Father Baker found himself now broke, but freer than he had ever been before.

Father Baker often dwelled on the miracles he had heard of while visiting the Our Lady Of Victory Shrine in France. He soon formulated a plan to empower people with the ability to help the orphaned children at St. Joseph's and St. John's. Father Baker wrote to postmasters across the nation with the request of some names and addresses of Catholic women who might be willing to donate 25 cents apiece to aid the children. He framed this request under the auspices of the newly formed "Our Lady Of Victory Association." Soon responses came in from all points on the compass, as folks were eager to help the good priest for such a worthy cause.

"Just as your purple balloon arrived with a tag on it, so too did so many kids arrive here with a tag around their neck when they got off of the train. They were kids that were abandoned and oftentimes abused and were thought to be a hopeless cause by many, but not by Father Baker," Msgr. Wurtz explained.

*(Courtesy of Frank Croisdale)*

*The Basilica.*

The boys, upwards of a thousand of them at one time, arrived at Limestone Hill to a world that most had long since given up hope of ever seeing again. Father Baker had demanded that all of the bars be taken off of the windows and that the rooms be rebuilt to affect a homier feel. Father Baker believed in the innate goodness of the "tough luck" kids and reinforced that belief by proclaiming "there are no bad boys."

In 1906, Father Baker announced plans to open a home for infants. Abandoned babies were often left at the doorsteps of Our Lady Of Victory and there was a real concern that there wasn't enough funding to properly care for them all. Father Baker put out an appeal for people to donate a crib and some bedding and, once again, his followers came through in spades. The new home featured a bassinet, just inside the front door, where someone could leave a baby that could not be properly cared for with no questions asked. Hundreds of people that would go on to live productive lives first met Father Baker in that fashion.

In 1921, Father Baker began work on what had been a life-long dream to honor the Blessed Mother in a grand fashion. He announced his plan to build a massive basilica in Lackawanna. Father Baker appealed to the faithful from across the land to send in $10 for a block of white marble for the basilica. The shrine was dedicated in May of 1926. The Vatican immediately anointed it as one of the finest shrines in the United States.

Father Nelson Baker passed into the realm of God on July 29, 1936. Nearly half a million people lined the streets during his wake and funeral. The Buffalo Times had this to say of a man that many believe should be elevated to Sainthood:

> *To have known Father Baker was to marvel at his energy and at the*
> *works that flowed from it. . . . To the hungry during his ministry he*
> *fed 50 million meals. During the depression at one time he was serving*
> *more than a million meals a year. He gave away a million loaves of bread.*
> *He clothed the naked to the number of a half million. He gave medical*
> *care to 250,000 and supplied medicines to 200,000 more. Three hundred*
> *thousand men, women, and children received some sort of education or*
> *training at his hands. A hundred thousand boys were trained for trades.*
> *Six hundred unmarried mothers in their distress knocked at his door and*
> *did not knock in vain. More than 6,000 destitute and abandoned babies*
> *were placed in foster homes. . . . .Men will give thanks that he lived*
> *and bless his memory.*

One of the greatest examples of Father Baker's generosity is detailed in the story of how he reacted to a theft of funds during the Great Depression. It was not uncommon for a postal clerk, struggling to make ends meet, to be tempted by the envelopes postmarked for Our Lady Of Victory. The postmen knew that behind the linen flap of the envelope more than likely lay a cash donation to one of Father Baker's causes.

One young clerk was caught red-handed and summarily fired. Father Baker received word of what had happened and summoned the man to appear before him. The fired clerk was brought into Father Baker's office expecting to be further reprimanded for his crime against the church. Imagine his surprise when the good Father not only absolved him of his sin, but also offered him a job at Our Lady Of Victory.

According to Beth Donovan, there are thousands of men who have lived rich lives that spent their formative years at one of the Our Lady Of Victory Institutions. These men, now fathers, grandfathers and even great-grandfathers, might have found themselves, under other circumstances, as being branded with a scarlet letter. The early part of the 20th century was a difficult time for kids with no parents. Instead of hanging their heads in shame, these men were afforded the opportunity to hold their heads high in knowing that they were part of an elite group of young men. They were "Father Baker's Boys."

*The work at Baker Victory Services continues today. To learn more, contact:*
*Baker Victory Services, 780 Ridge Road, Lackawanna, N. Y. 14218, (716) 828-9500,*
*www.bakervictoryservices.org*

# *Memorials Honor Two Lives Taken Too Soon*

*There comes to me out of the Past,*
*A voice, whose tones are sweet and wild,*
*Singing a song almost divine,*
*And with a tear in every line.*
–Longfellow

Two people, two lives, two tragedies, two memorials.

Less than a mile apart, they stand as a reminder of two of Niagara Falls' greatest assets, its youth, taken from this world without warning and without mercy.

The first memorial is at the on ramp to the I-190 from Niagara Falls Boulevard near 66th Street. It was there on the late afternoon of October 6, 2003, that 21-year-old Mark Kirkpatrick was killed when his motorcycle collided with a van. The second is on the 66th Street pedestrian overpass above the LaSalle Expressway. On December 14, 2002, three young males viciously murdered Jennifer Bolender in that location.

For Mark Kirkpatrick's family and friends some closure was afforded when his body was laid to rest. Jennifer Bolender's family took a big step forward when the three males accused of her murder were found guilty and sentenced to lengthy prison terms.

For the families and friends of Jennifer and Mark, that may have been the easy part. Having things to focus on, a funeral or a trial, occupies the mind. Nothing can quite prepare a young person for the reality of having to face his or her own mortality by dealing with the death of a friend. Just as nothing can truly comfort a parent who must bury his or her own child, as these words from Shakespeare's King John, Act iii, Scene 4 can attest to:

*Grief fills up the room of my absent child,*
*Lies in his bed, walks up and down with me,*
*Puts on his pretty looks, repeats his words,*
*Remembers me all of his gracious parts,*
*Stuffs out his vacant garments with his form.*

One way in which both sets of people have begun to cope is by establishing the two memorials in honor of their lost loved ones. At each memorial, there are an assortment of flowers and crosses. Three candles burn at Jennifer's memorial and someone has carved a pumpkin that reads "We Love You Mark" at Kirkpatrick's memorial.

There is also a poem on display at each of the memorials. A friend of Jennifer's tries to create couplets that will find some sense in her brutal murder, while a relative of Mark's laments the fact that she didn't say, "I love you," the last time she saw him alive.

*(Courtesy of Lorena L. Lee)*

*Mark Kirkpatrick.*

One of the least focused-upon aspects of tragedy is the emotional aftermath that surviving relatives and friends must cope with after someone has been suddenly and permanently taken away. When the three young males implicated in the murder were sentenced to prison, one couldn't help but be happy for the family and friends of Jennifer Bolender. Sending those murderers to jail for even a thousand years will not bring that innocent young girl back to life, but it may ease just an ounce of the pain being felt by friends who miss her laughter and parents who can only hold her in their memories. And for that, we, as a community, must find a small amount of solace to embrace and nurture.

In times like these it is not uncommon for people embroiled in grief to turn to their religion for insight and for comfort. It is also not uncommon for religion to offer little in the way of either, at least in a tangible fashion. What the world's major religions have to offer us as it pertains to understanding such senseless loss is one important and powerful five-letter word – faith.

And that's just as it should be. How can we expect to ever make sense of the loss of lives so young and so innocent? The understanding of such events lies somewhere far beyond the comprehension of man. What can be understood is the healing effect that a heartfelt memorial can bring.

In preparing to write this story, my family and I visited the memorials for Jennifer and Mark. It is difficult to describe the sea of emotions that overcomes you as you stand on the ground, now made sacred, where a young man and a young lady perished from this Earth.

As I watched my 2-year-old son lean in to smell the flowers, I was graphically reminded of how fleeting life and youth can be.

"There but for the grace of God go I," is an oft-quoted phrase, and for good reason. It could just have easily been my child, or yours, that hopped on his motorcycle to go for a spin that he would return in a body bag from. It also could have easily been one of our daughters that went moonlight bowling and did not find safe passage on an overpass that she'd traversed hundreds of time before.

In fact, it was.

Due to a decrease in citizenry, Niagara Falls, not unlike most Western New York cities, has become more of a large town. With large town sensibilities. One of a town's greatest attributes is its sense of community. We shop at the same stores, read the same newspapers, watch the same television channels, eat at the same restaurants and vote for the same politicians. Is it too much of a stretch to think of our children as a shared asset as well?

When Hillary Clinton wrote the words, "It takes a village," she could have been speaking directly to Niagara Falls and the importance of the two memorials that shadow 66th Street. Those two tragic events took from the soul of this village and it is the soul of this village that will aid in the healing of two grieving families.

I know of no large gesture that any of us can undertake to help right that which has been wronged. We cannot turn back the hands of time, nor can we bring back those that have crossed over to a higher plane. But, I do know of a thousand small gestures that we can make that will help preserve the memory of Jennifer Bolender and Mark Kirkpatrick.

Should you pass those memorials let them remind you to hug your kids and tell them that you love them, each and every time you or they leave home. Let it remind you that there are people on the streets of this city that need your charity and not your condemnation. Let it remind you that a simple act, like holding a door open for an elder or shoveling the snow for a shut-in, pays dividends far more valuable than money. And may it remind you that each day will provide you with opportunities to prove yourself more noble and charitable than even you thought that you could be.

If that comes to pass, then it will be true that, like a phoenix rising from the ashes, so too can good arise from such tragedy.

A search of Jennifer's name on a search engine brought up this posting by Stephanie Kamp on a pen-pal bulletin board dated from August 16, 2002.

*If you are or know any of these people..PLEASE email me right away. I really*
*wanted to get back in contact with them. Thank you so much.*

Among the handful of names she listed was this one – Jennifer Bolender. The irony of her words is that they've now become a sentiment shared by everyone in this community who loved and was befriended by Jennifer and Mark.

Two people, two lives, two tragedies, two memorials.

Both taken from us too young, too soon.

# *Vacationing Fire Chief Saves Lives Of Ontario Family*

*Chance favors only the prepared mind.*
–Louis Pasteur

P eople often talk about someone being "at the wrong place, at the wrong time." You're likely to hear those words spoken when someone is detailing the unfortunate fate of a car jacking or drive-by shooting victim.

Is there a flip side to that coin? Can someone be "at the right place, at the right time"? Ask that question of the Yellow family of Lewiston, New York, and you'll get a very quick and very decisive "yes."

For years the Shiah family of Niagara Falls have made it a yearly ritual to spend Memorial Day weekend at their cabin in Dunville, Ontario. On Friday, May 28th, 1988, they set out, as they'd done for so many years, to beat the holiday rush across the Rainbow Bridge into Canada.

"We got to the Rainbow Bridge and traffic was backed up for miles, so we tried the Whirlpool Bridge and it was more of the same," Rick Shiah said from the kitchen table of a home on Cayuga Island, in Niagara Falls, that's been in the Shiah family for decades. "For the only time that I can remember, we turned around and went back home with the intent of getting an early start to beat the traffic the next morning."

Saturday morning the Shiahs, Rick, his wife, Kathy, their son, Aaron, and friend Michael Burke, found the bridge to be smooth sailing and took the scenic Fonthill Road route up to their cottage. As the Shiahs were enjoying the car ride to their cottage respite, Rick noticed a fire burning up in the distance.

"At first I thought that it was a trash fire, but it seemed a bit too close to the road for that. As we approached the intersection it became apparent that what was on fire was a vehicle, a Chevy Blazer I think it was, and an attached trailer," Rick explained.

Now is probably a good time in the story to give you the background of Mr. Shiah. A Vietnam Veteran who served with the 4th Infantry, in 1988 Rick was 18 years into a decorated career with the Niagara Falls Fire Department. He was, at the time, a battalion chief and would retire in 1997 as Fire Chief. It also is important to note that Kathy was an experienced registered nurse.
The vehicle was partially in the ditch with the driver's side facing down.

"There was a parking lot for a business where the vehicle was and there must have been at least 20 people standing around. At first, I told Rick to just keep going because they must have it under control," Kathy explained.

The fireman inside Rick told him that he better take a closer look, just to be sure. What he saw would shock him to his very core.

"When I got out, there was a male with a portable radio in his hand and I figured he was a volunteer firefighter of some sort. I was about to explain to him who I was when he said, 'Just keep back, there's nothing you can do.' The way that he said it, I knew that there must be people trapped inside the vehicle," Rick said.

*(Courtesy of Richard Shiah)*

**Richard Shiah.**

At this time both the trailer and the back of the Blazer were on fire. Rick's years of fire training took over and he approached the vehicle with the wind at his back. The passenger side window was opened and he could see the driver slumped over. Battling the intense heat, Rick looked into the back seat and, to his horror, saw two young boys trapped there crying.

"I could see small fires erupting on the floor around the boys," Rick explained. "I'd removed my T-shirt and used it to grip the door handle to try and pry it open."

The intense heat drove the fire chief back, where he formulated another plan of attack.

"I told Kathy and Aaron that there were three people trapped in the vehicle and my son retrieved a denim jacket from our car and I put it on and went back in," Rick detailed.

Rick was able to reach in and retrieve the youngest boy, a 5-year-old named Maurice Yellow, from the burning Blazer.

"As I pulled him out, his hair began to catch fire, I ran him back to Kathy and Aaron who put out the spot fires on him," Rick said.

The onlookers watched on in stunned silence. Rick yelled to the crowd to find a garden hose, but none was found.

As Rick approached the burning vehicle once more, he was startled to hear repeated "whoosh" sounds.

"I thought that it was the tires exploding, which would have been odd because they normally hold out much longer into a fire. I wasn't worried about the gas tank exploding – people who aren't firefighters often think that the gas tank will blow immediately, but that's rarely the case," said Rick.

What the fire chief didn't know was that the Yellow family had been on their way to the racetrack and there was a racecar and containers of racing fuel on the trailer. The "whoosh" sound was the racing fuel combusting. Time was now truly of the essence.

By this time, 8-year-old Manny Yellow leaned over the front seat and had wrapped his arms around the neck of his unconscious father – refusing to let go. Rick called to the unaware driver, in vain, to open his door. Suddenly, the fiberglass roof of the Blazer began to melt and the inside cabin filled with thick, black smoke. Unable to see or continue to bear the oppressing heat, Rick once again retreated.

"At that moment I felt terrible. I remember thinking here I am a firefighter and my family is going to witness about the worst thing you could ever see, a family burning alive in a fire," Rick explained.

Rick tried to prepare his family for the worst and told his wife Kathy, "I can't get to them, they're going to die."

Going against his instincts, Rick approached the Blazer from the ditch side; it was the same side to which the wind was blowing.

"I had no choice at that point, I wasn't going to reach them from the other side," Rick said.

Standing on grass that was on fire, with explosions echoing in his ears, Rick approached the driver's side door praying for a miracle. The angels were listening.

"Just as I was reaching for the door, it opened and the father and little boy came tumbling out. Whether the father regained consciousness long enough to work the handle, I'll never know, but thank goodness that it happened," Rick explained.

The dad and his oldest son were both burned much more extensively than little Maurice had been.

"I grabbed the boy and tossed him up the embankment and the father and I were able to scramble through the burning grass to safety," Rick said.
Suddenly Kathy was running a triage unit as she, Aaron and Michael used a 5-gallon jug of water they had in the car to treat the wounds of the victims.

"I wasn't cooling down very well and was feeling a little light-headed. However, I was over-come by a feeling of euphoria. This was something that was going to be really bad, as bad as it gets, and instead it turned into something wonderful," Shiah explained.

The Yellows were taken by ambulance to a Canadian hospital and eventually all made complete recoveries. Rick, Kathy and Aaron drove back to Sheehan Memorial Hospital in Buffalo, where Rick was admitted and treated for one week.

The man with the mobile radio who told Rick to stay back was not a volunteer firefighter, but an imposter posing as an emergency official. He was arrested by Canadian police and convicted of impersonating a public official. His actions very nearly cost a family their lives.

To this day, the Yellows and the Shiahs remain close friends, often spending holidays and special events together. The Canadian government honored Rick Shiah with the prestigious Star of Courage Award for his heroic actions that day. The Yellow family, who are Native Americans, have made Rick an honorary member of the Turtle Clan.

"I'm not sure if what happened can be called a miracle. What still gets me is the timing, for 40 years, we'd gone to our cottage, never once having turned back. If we had gotten there (at the scene of the accident) five minutes later, it would have been too late. Only someone with years of fire training could have gotten those people out of there alive, of that I am certain," Rick said.

Sounds like a job made for the right person at the right time.

# *Thankfully, North Tonawanda Man Spent Life Going Around In Circles*

*Once around is never enough.*
–Herschell Carrousel Museum Motto

Usually when people talk about going around in circles they are referring to something negative. Moving in a straight line is euphemistic for progress, while moving in a circular fashion connotes wasted effort or stagnation.

Whoever coined that phrase must never have spent time on a carousel. A spin on the wooden horses is anything but wasted time. While riding an elm-carved steed one can be transported back to a simpler time. One where men were chivalrous, ladies demure and the town faire filled the summer air with sounds of joy. Twirling on an authentic carousel of yore can give one a literal understanding of its often used synonym – merry-go-round.

The late 19th and early 20th centuries saw the golden era for carousel manufacturing. North Tonawanda was at the epicenter of the newfound industry of amusement rides and one man stood as its King - Allan Herschell.

In 1873, Herschell was a partner in the Armitage Herschell Company, a manufacturer of farm equipment and steam engines. The company began manufacturing carousels as a sideline. Because of America's instant love for the new inventions, carousels quickly became 50% of Armitage Herschell's sales and the company briskly began to move away from the farm equipment industry. The firm began producing a line of traveling rides powered by steam engines.

I learned all of this while talking with Elizabeth Schutt, curator of the Herschell Museum at her office on a freakishly cold, even by Buffalo standards, January morning.

"All of the early rides were for adults only," Schutt said. "They felt that they were too fast and dangerous for kids in those days. I love telling that to kids who visit the museum today. Kids who were raised on Disney and high-speed, gravity-defying rides. They just can't fathom that they wouldn't have been allowed on the carousel."

In 1899, Armitage and Herschell go their separate ways and Herschell soon forms a new company with the Spillman brothers. This new company begins to experiment with menagerie animals on the carousels. In place of horses, riders could hop on frogs, zebras, even kangaroos.

"The kangaroos are the one animal that makes the most sense to me," Schutt said. "They actually go up and down in real life. Of course, on the carousel they have them stationary, go figure."

*(Courtesy of Herschell Carrousel Factory)*

*One of Alan Herschell's carousels.*

In 1913, Alan Herschell retires and the Spillman brothers carry on with a new factory on the corner of Goundry and Oliver Streets in North Tonawanda. Today, that corner is home to the Carousel Apartments, named in honor of the factory that once stood in their place.

After three years of retirement, Herschell's wife, Ida (Spillman - sister to Allan's former partners) decides that he's driving her crazy around the house and urges him to go back to work. Herschell concurs and buys an old lumberyard on Thompson Street just three blocks from the Spillman factory and spends the next 30-odd years in fierce competition with his old mates.

During this period the two companies accuse one another of stealing customers, ideas and employees. In a smaller scale version of Ford versus General Motors, both firms enjoy booming businesses, but always keep one eye glued to the actions of the other.

"The only time that they put aside their differences was for the betterment of the country during the Second World War," Schutt explained. "Both companies had a surplus of rides that couldn't be shipped due to the outbreak of the war. So they had all of these rides in their stock and were sitting there saying, 'What are we going to do we these?' So, what they did was have war bond fairs. They would jointly set up the rides in an area park and instead of having people buy tickets for a ride, they'd have them buy war bonds."

In 1923, Alan Herschell passed away and his company would eventually change hands many times before being purchased by Chance Manufacturing and moved to Wichita, Kansas, in 1969.

The story of the carousel's connection to North Tonawanda may have ended there if not for a group of concerned citizens who refused to let that historical part of the city's past die.

The Carousel Society of the Niagara Frontier was formed in 1982 and the group fixed its sights on buying one of Allan Herschell's original carousels and returning it back to use in North Tonawanda. The cost of purchasing the carousel was tens of thousands of dollars and the group set out to earn it, penny by penny.

"They had ice cream socials, card parties and white elephant sales. Local kids brought pennies in and donated them. They sold ride tickets before they even had the machine. Allan Herschell, grandson of the company founder, was very instrumental in getting things going at that time," Schutt said.

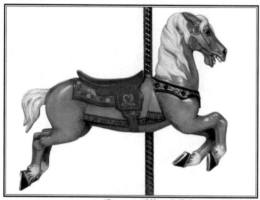

*(Courtesy of Herschell Carrousel Factory)*

**Restored hand-carved carousel pony.**

The society began scouring the earth for Herschell carousels that may be obtainable and finally found just what they were looking for in a carousel from 1916. The ride was one of the first three produced by the Thompson Street factory and was up for auction in Canada.

"If you want to confuse the people at customs, tell them that you're bringing a carousel in a thousand pieces through," Schutt said.

Once it was back, the process began of bringing it up to code. Because it had never operated in the United States, it needed electrical work, much cleaning and some new gears to get cleared for operation by New York State.

"Now that they had the carousel, they needed a place to house it and saw the old roundhouse (at the Thompson Street site) and were delighted to find it unoccupied. The roundhouse was leased and the carousel was finally home," said Schutt.

Soon the society began to realize that there was a great story to be told about the Allan Herschell factory. Not only had it been a major employer in Western New York, but also led the way in development of kiddie rides for all of America.

"The society realized that the Thompson Street factory was the last standing in the country that had manufactured carousels and kiddie rides. They first raised money to purchase it and, once it was secured, began to raise money to stabilize the structure," Schutt said.

The group hit a setback when one of the Niagara Frontier's famous winter snowstorms dropped so much of the white stuff that the roundhouse collapsed. Fortunately, the carousel was not under it at the time. Because the building is registered as a National Historic Landmark, rebuilding wasn't as easy as hiring an architect to draw up a new design.

"We had to recreate it, exactly as it was in 1916," Elizabeth explained. "We were able to save one wall and one ceiling panel. The rest was painstakingly recreated using historic photographs. Often people ask, 'What are the chains hanging from the ceiling?' That's 1916 air-conditioning technology. They open the windows. Even those were restored just as they were in 1916."

The museum has been opened to the public for the past 14 years. Approximately 20,000 visitors come through each year and learn of the storied past of carousels in North Tonawanda. Folks can interact with pony carvers and even try their own hand at equine work working. The society, which started with 10 members, has grown to over 400 from all points on the globe. There are 70 volunteers that are heavily involved in the day-to-day operation of the museum.

"We couldn't even begin to exist without those (volunteers)," Schutt said.

The society now has officially purchased the Herschell Company from Chance Manufacturing. They now supplement the costs of operating the museum by supplying parts for all remaining Herschell amusement rides that are still in operation worldwide. Of the approximately 148 vintage carousels still operating, nearly half of them were made in Western New York.

The 1916 carousel that operates at the museum is 40 feet in diameter and sports 36 hand-carved horses and 580 lights. A Wurlitzer military band organ from 1910 adds the soundtrack as riders are merrily spun in circle after circle.

"A lot of kids have only been on carousels that move really slow, somewhere like 2-3 revolutions per minute. I love the look on their faces when they get off of ours and have traveled at 6.5 r.p.m. Suddenly they realize just where the term thrill ride came from," said Schutt.

"When I tell them that in 1916, the steam engine that powered this carousel moved it at somewhere around 8 revolutions per minute, but state law doesn't allow it to go that fast anymore, you can see their minds working and saying 'Wow,'"

One thing you can be sure of is that tens of thousands of Western New Yorkers will continue to be transported back to a simpler time at the Herschell Carrousel Factory Museum. As smiling parents pack giddy children back into their cars after going for a spin on one of Allan Herschell's gifts of fun to the world, they will leave with a better understanding of the museum's motto: "Once around is not enough."

*To learn more about the Herschell Carrousel Factory Museum, contact:*
*The Herschell Carrousel Factory Museum, 180 Thompson Street, North Tonawanda, NY 14120*
*(716) 693-1885*

# Jewish Merchant's Kind Gesture Saves Niagara University

*Two friends, two bodies with one soul inspir'd.*
–Homer

Usually when we hear a story concerning two religions, it is one filled with conflict and violence. Whether it is Catholics and Protestants in Northern Ireland or Jews and Muslims on the Gaza Strip, religions usually mix like oil and water, with disharmony being the end result.

That's what makes this next story about a Jewish store owner and a Vincentian priest so special. Not only were the two men of different faiths friends, but their friendship saved what is now one of Western New York's finest institutions of learning.

What we know today as Niagara University was founded in 1856 as Our Lady of Angels seminary. The school dedicated to the pursuit of higher learning was started on a shoestring budget and struggled mightily to stay out of the red.

As the mid-part of the 19th century gave way to the last, Father Michael Cavanaugh was named procurator and treasurer of Our Lady of Angels. Father Mike was a witty and jovial man and was well respected by not only the students at the seminary, but by the denizens of the Niagara Frontier as well.

Father Mike's work often took him to a section of the current city of Niagara Falls that was at that time known as the hamlet of Suspension Bridge.

One of Father Mike's favorite stops in Suspension Bridge was at the supply store known as "Brown's Dry Goods and Clothier."

The owner of "Brown's Dry Goods and Clothier" was a young Jewish immigrant by the name of Marcus Brown. Marcus had worked his way up from a merchant's apprentice and used the store's profits to supply a home for himself and his widowed mother.

Father Mike had been taking his business to Marcus Brown since those early days when Marcus was just an apprentice. Marcus Brown's ubiquitous smile and easy demeanor had endeared him to Father Mike and the two men had long since moved past the limiting relationship of buyer and seller into the unrestricting realm of friendship.

When Father Mike would visit the store for supplies and find that his needs outweighed the spending power of his purse – which was often – something amazing would happen. When Marcus Brown would tally up the purchase, it would "miraculously" equal the exact amount of coin residing in Father Mike's purse. Once the priest had left the store, Marcus Brown would reach into his own pocket to balance the till.

Although you'd think that a Jewish shop owner would be the last person that a Vincentian priest would confide in about his fears concerning the financial state of his seminary, you'd be quite incorrect. The friendship that the two men shared bridged the gap between their different beliefs and each became the other's closest confidant.

In the winter of 1882 came the watershed moment that Father Mike had long feared. The seminary's debt had been steadily rising. While its income was stalled, Father Mike was talented with making due with limited finances and had set aside just enough money to appease everyone while the seminary held on for a financial breakthrough.

Just when it looked like the seminary would weather the storm, disaster struck. The seminary's mortgage holder, Judge DeVeaux's estate, demanded total debt owed it by our Lady of Angels, a whopping $3,000, to be paid in full. When the seminary replied that it didn't have the funds, an immediate foreclosure was called for and a sheriff's auction of the seminary and all of its possessions was set for the following Saturday at 10.

The Seminarians at Our Lady of Angels held round-the-clock prayer vigils and asked for divine intervention to save the learning institute. One day before the scheduled sheriff's auction, a massive snowstorm hit the Niagara Frontier rendering most roads impassable. The president of the seminary took the blizzard as an act of mercy from God, one designed to spare the seminary from auction. Father Mike was inclined to think so too, but decided to hedge his bet with a visit to his old friend Marcus Brown.

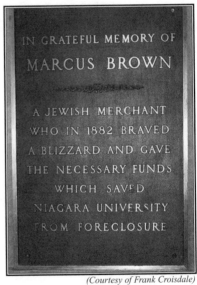

*(Courtesy of Frank Croisdale)*
**Plaque that hangs inside the student center at Niagara University.**

Father Mike found it quite difficult to navigate his way through the snowstorm to get to Brown's Dry Goods and Clothier. Once there he detailed the seminary's impending doom to his good friend. Marcus listened intently. When Father Mike was through, Marcus told him not to worry and that the seminary would not stand alone in its hour of need.

At daybreak on Saturday morning the snowstorm was showing no signs of relenting. For Marcus Brown, it was the dawn of the most holy day of the week, the Jewish Sabbath, and he vowed to let God's strength carry him to the aid of his friend Father Mike.
Marcus set out on foot to make the three-mile trek from his store to our Lady of Angels Seminary. While the wind howled and the snow blew Marcus Brown made his way along the

treacherous path that wound its way along the top of the Niagara Gorge. Because all of the fences that served as guide marks were buried in snow, there was a real danger of putting down a false step and falling to a certain death into the nearly 200-foot high gorge. Marcus fought against the oftentimes shoulder-deep snow with all of his might. When he began to fear that he might freeze to death in his own perspiration the thought of his kind friend in need brought warmth to his soul.

At 9:45 A.M. the sheriff arrived at the seminary and stole whatever hope remained that the snowstorm would cancel the auction. As the morning neared the ever-dreaded 10 o'clock deadline, Father Mike said one last prayer.

Just then the seminary doors crashed open and a half-frozen Marcus Brown collapsed into a chair before the startled onlookers. Exhausted and near delirium, Marcus pulled a checkbook from his pocket and whispered to Father Mike to make the amount payable for the full amount due the mortgage company.

Our Lady of Angels was saved!

Today, Niagara University has an annual enrollment of approximately 2,500 undergraduate students pursuing degrees from 30 different departments.

The school is held in high regard not only for its academic standards, but also for its Vincentian teachings of compassion and generosity.

Before he died Marcus Brown was asked by an interviewer if he'd received any interest on the money that he'd loaned Our Lady of Angels.

Indignant at the mere suggestion of any financial gain from his generosity, Marcus Brown answered the question with these words, "What, ask Father Mike for interest? Why, no. Was he not my friend?"

The moral of this story is that the best type of debt is one that can never be repaid. The bond of friendship between a Jewish store owner and a Jesuit priest continues to pay dividends to thousands of college kids each and every year.

# Former Buffalo Bills Player Survives 9/11 Scare During Heart Transplant Surgery

*For remember, my sentimental friend, a heart is not judged by how much you love, but by how much you are loved by others.*
–L. Frank Baum

**A**sk any American of a certain age what they were doing when Pearl Harbor was bombed and they'll answer without hesitation. The same holds true for the day J.F.K. was assassinated. September 11, 2001 is a date that has been added to that infamous list. The amazing story that follows, concerning a former Buffalo Bills player's experience of 9/11, proves that the loyalty forged between teammates on the football field endures long after the final whistle
is blown.

Fullback may be the most under appreciated position in all of football. While the halfback gets all of the carries and all of the glory, the fullback is usually only recognized by his teammates and, if he's good, by his foes. It is the job of a fullback to power into a hole created by the offensive line and collide into a charging linebacker in order to free the halfback to gain yardage.

Doug Goodwin was a fullback for the Buffalo Bills from 1965-68. In the days before the merger between the National and American Football Leagues, it was common for players to be drafted by clubs from each of the two entities. The Packers selected Doug in the 5th round of the NFL draft, while the Bills tabbed him in the 11th round on the AFL's selection day.

"I chose the Bills because they gave a better bonus," Goodwin, now 62, said by telephone from his home on Long Island. "Also, there was a lot of racial tension in the country at that time and Green Bay had very few blacks. Buffalo was well integrated, I felt at home there."

Goodwin joined the Bills at the height of their dominance of the AFL. With a team filled with high-caliber players like Jack Kemp, Booker Edgerson, Ed Rutkowski, Billy Shaw, Charley Ferguson, Tom Day and Paul Maguire, the Bills would become repeat champions of the AFL during Goodwin's rookie season.

After leaving the Bills, Doug played for the Falcons, Packers and Colts before hanging up his cleats for good. Doug began a career as a high school math teacher and also dedicated himself to participating in drug programs designed to aid kids most at risk of becoming addicts. "I was working in District 6 in Manhattan. At that time District 6 was the headquarters for drugs in New York City. Walking down the street there was like walking down a supermarket aisle for drug purchases. Whatever you wanted, someone was there selling it. It meant a lot to me to know that, as a counselor, I helped some kids stay clear of all of that," Doug explained. In the early 1990s, Doug began experiencing pain in his side. Still possessing the type of macho man mentality that had carried him through his football career, Doug was reluctant to disclose his pain to his wife, Gwen, or their son, Doug Jr.

"I was looking out for my son," Goodwin told me. "My mind was on him and not on myself. At first, I refused to go to the hospital and then when I did eventually go, I checked out twice."

When Goodwin finally checked into the hospital and stayed for testing, doctors told him that he had an enlarged heart, three times the normal size, that was pumping blood at a greatly diminished rate. In 1993, Goodwin's heart was connected to an implanted defibrillator and the retired ball player received an up-close and personal look at his own mortality.

"They hit me with it about 12 times. I never felt that type of pain before ever in my life. My lungs were punctured and I had to wait four days in critical condition for a new defibrillator," Doug told me.

*(Courtesy of Gwendolyn W. Goodwin)*
**Doug Goodwin.**

By 2001, things had deteriorated to the point where doctors determined that the only thing that was going to extend Doug Goodwin's life was a heart transplant. Unfortunately, Doug had three strikes working against him, his size, 6'2" and nearly 300 pounds, eliminated 95% of donated hearts because they would be too small to pump blood though his body, his rare blood type would eliminate a large percentage of those hearts that were large enough and his minimal health insurance would not cover the high cost of the surgery.

It was during this period that one of Doug's doctors at Presbyterian Hospital initiated a sequence of events that resulted in him being alive today.

"He was a German doctor and he saw my 1965 Bills' championship ring. He asked me if I was an athlete and I told him I played pro football. Somehow, and I don't know to this day how he did it, but he called Ralph Wilson at his house. Before I knew what was happening, the Bills came to my rescue," Doug explained.

Ralph Wilson reached into his own wallet and helped defray some of Doug's mounting medical expenses. Gwen, along with, Doug's former teammate Charlie Ferguson organized a surprise birthday party for Doug and invited a bunch of the players from the 1965 championship team,

along with players from Doug's high school and college squads.
"It was great to see all of those guys again. Jack Kemp volunteered to pay for my entire
operation himself," Doug said. "I couldn't believe it, he was back as captain of the old team
again, ready to lead us into battle one more time."

Before Doug could take up his old quarterback on his most generous offer, Ralph Wilson and
the Bills called with some good news. Doug was eligible for financial relief through the NFL
Players Association Trust, and its Dire Need Fund. Doug was hospitalized and the wait for a
suitable heart was on.

In the wee-wee hours of September 11, 2001 word was sent to Doug not to eat anything
because his new heart had been found. The surgery was scheduled for 9 o'clock.

As amazing as Doug's journey had been up to that point, he would have to survive one last
and most unexpected turn of events. Doug's heart was being flown in from Logan Airport in
Boston, the same airport from which terrorists were boarding airplanes that they would fly
into the World Trade Center buildings.

Reporter Bob Glauber of Newsday was able to connect the dots of what happened that morning
and offer a compelling look at the interconnected paths of the terrorists' actions and Doug's
new heart.

Glauber states that Doug's heart left Logan at 7:50 A.M., at 7:59, terrorists departed, using
the same runway, on the first plane that would be rerouted to the World Trade Centers.

The heart landed at Teterboro Airport in New Jersey, 11 minutes later the terrorists fly their
airplane into the World Trade Center. An ambulance carrying Doug's heart crossed the
George Washington Bridge into NYC at 9:15. Six minutes later all bridges into new York
were closed.

At 9:30 A.M., Doug's surgery began and five-hours later, the former Buffalo Bill had a new
heart pumping blood throughout his veins.
"I didn't wake up until the next day and I had no idea (that the attack on America) had happened.
My wife had gone home the night before (the surgery) to get some rest and she wasn't able to
get back into the city for three days," Doug explained.

Goodwin recalls looking up at a television showing the aftermath of the bombings and not
understanding what he was seeing.

"I thought it was a Godzilla movie, I couldn't believe it was real," Goodwin said.

Eventually, Doug learned of the full extent of the attacks on our nation and of how close he
came to not receiving his new heart. When he was asked whom he is most thankful for in his
life, he did not hesitate with his answer, "God and the love of my family – that's what got me
through. Beyond that, I don't know where I'd be without the Buffalo Bills. Of all the teams

that I played for, they were the only ones to step up. I had no idea in 1965 that I was getting teammates for life. I sure made the right decision by not going with Green Bay."
The one Buffalo Bill closest to Doug Goodwin's heart, both the old one and the new, is team owner Ralph Wilson.

"Here's a story about Ralph Wilson that you can put in your book," Doug said. "When I was a rookie we practiced out in Blasdell. I had just run a play and knelt down on one knee by the snow fence that separated the spectators from the players to catch my breath. Some of the fans had come around the fence and this one guy, dressed in some natty clothes, walked up to me and said, 'Good play.' I looked up at him and said, 'Not now, man. I'm too tired to give you an autograph.' He just looked at me and laughed and walked back to the other side of the fence. At dinner that night, (Bills Head Coach) Lou Saban said, 'Gentlemen, I'd like to introduce you to your owner, Mr. Ralph Wilson,' and out walks the guy that I told not to ask me for an autograph. I just about died. I've talked to him about it since then and he got a big kick out of it. I tell you, I love that man so much. Even though I was a role player for just three years he treated me like I was an all-star."

Because of the actions of an owner with a heart of gold and teammates who never forgot one of their own, the new heart inside Doug Goodwin's chest beats with blood that's not only red, but also blue and white, the die-hard colors of the Buffalo Bills.

*To make a donation to help with Doug's ongoing medical costs, please send a check or money order to:*
*Doug "Mackey" Goodwin Heart Trust Fund, Bank Of South Carolina, 256 Meeting Street, Charleston, SC 29401*

# Buffalo Man Gives His Brother A Very Special Gift – The Gift Of Life

*There is a destiny which makes us brothers;*
*None goes his way alone.*
–Edwin Markham

"**I** am my brother's keeper" are words that are often spoken metaphorically. The intent is that we all owe a debt to our fellow man to look out for one another's best interests and well-being. For Marty Giles, the words took on a very literal definition when he gave his brother Rob a most special gift – the gift of life.

"My brother Rob's always been the responsible one while I've been more of the prodigal son," Marty explained over coffee at a Tim Hortons in North Tonawanda. "While I was galli-vanting around in California he was here going to college and then working hard at a career."

While in his early 20s, Rob, now 37, was diagnosed with a severe intestinal disorder known as Ulcerative Colitis. While the illness gave the Giles family cause for concern, everyone was quite certain that Rob would overcome it with minimal difficulty.

Things didn't get better for Rob, however, and five years after his initial diagnosis he needed to have major surgery. Doctors would remove just about all of Rob's intestines.

"Throughout all of these times of being so severely sick, Rob continued to work and to go to school. What was so amazing was that his outlook and demeanor never changed," Marty explained.

Rob recovered from the surgery and was feeling better than he had in years. Just when the Giles family began feeling comfortable that Rob's medical problems were behind him, tragedy hit.

In 2000, about a year after the intestinal surgery, Rob went in for a check-up and the doctors discovered that he had Primary Sclerosis Meningitis (PSM) – a disease that is often linked with the Colitis that had caused Rob's intestinal problems. PSM causes the ducts in the liver to harden; as a result the body can't process water. The disease is both painful and, without a liver transplant, fatal.

Rob's health deteriorated quickly. He was in tremendous pain, his eyes became jaundiced and, eventually, the water that his liver could no longer process began pooling in his legs. At this time Marty was working in Rochester, NY, as a kitchen manager for the TGIF restau-rant chain. His car became a frequent sight on the NYS Thruway, as he would often clock out of work and race back to Buffalo to be at his brother's side.

"At that time my life was going really well, with promotions at work and things like that, and my brother's life was falling apart around him. I started to feel really guilty, partly because I had my health while my brother was losing his, and partly because I wasn't in Buffalo to help him," Marty explained.

Rob was put onto the National Registry to be a recipient of a liver for a transplant. According to figures posted at ustransplant.org only 25% of people in need of a liver transplant receive one within 5 months of being placed on the registry. They then must hope that the donated liver is a match. The Giles family feared that Rob didn't have that long to wait.

"By this time the water in Rob's legs was really bad. His legs and feet swelled up to the point where his feet were like footballs. We couldn't find shoes big enough to fit him so we had to remove the laces and cut the shoes open with a razor blade so Rob could wear them," Marty said.

The Gileses knew that Rob was in a race against the clock, one that he was running a real chance of losing. Right about that time, Marty became aware of a surgical procedure that was in its infancy. The Cleveland Clinic, where Rob was being treated, was pioneering a new procedure whereby a person could donate a portion of his or her liver to be transplanted into someone else. The living donor procedure is possible because the liver is the only human organ that can regenerate itself. After talking it over with his mother, Marty came to a decision. He was going to give Rob part of his liver.

*(Courtesy of Martin Giles)*
**Rob and Marty Giles.**

"It was very simple to me, really," Marty said.
"My brother, my best friend, was dying and I wasn't going to sit idly by when there was something I could do about it. Once I make my mind up, I'm pretty stubborn about things."

Marty, who kept himself in top physical condition and who once had bicycled across America solo just for the challenge was now going to put his own life at risk to help save Rob's.

At that time the living donor program was in its infancy. The good news was that 80% of all donors survived the operation fine, the bad news being that 20% left their lives on the operating room table. Those odds gave Marty cause for concern, but never cause for reconsideration of his decision.

Marty called his boss at TGIF's and broke the news that he would need months off for the surgery.

"I can't say enough about TGIF's. Not only did they understand and support my decision, my district manager, Joe Nichols, shifted people's schedules and brought managers in from other cities to cover my shifts. They kept me on full salary for the entire time I was out," Marty explained.

Marty was sent to the Cleveland Clinic for a number of pre-operation tests. Aside from taking enough vials of blood to fill the refrigerators at the Red Cross, the medical staff at the Cleveland Clinic put Marty through a battery of tests, including an intense psychological probe.

"One of the questions they asked me was, 'Why do you want to do this?' I said, 'To save my brother, of course, and that I felt the need to do something special in my life to make right with God and with my family and that saving Rob's life will allow me to fulfill that need.' I asked them, 'Does that make me sound selfish?' The psychiatrist said, 'No, in fact that's the most honest answer I've ever received to that question.'"

Marty was assigned a liver transplant coordinator, Lou Farquhar. She would guide him through each step of the transplant process. Lou told Marty that the procedure he was about to undergo was more complicated than a double lung and heart transplant. Fortunately, Marty's stubborn nature ushered those words in one ear and out the other as he already had his mind locked on the business of saving his brother's life.

The pre-tests showed that Marty's liver was a 50% match for compatibility for Rob. A 25% match is doable, so 50% was cause for celebration.

Finally the surgery date was set for late July 2001. Marty took his leave from TGIF's a month before the surgery to get both his mind and body ready for the ordeal that lay ahead.

"I prayed every day, asking God for strength. Physically, I've always been in good shape but I began working out and running each day to get in the best shape of my life," Marty confided.

The day before the surgery was to have taken place, one of the surgeons had a medical emergency and the operation was rescheduled for August 2nd.

A caravan of friends and family traveled with the Giles family to Cleveland. Marty's good friend Paul kept his mind at ease by playing Trivial Pursuit with Marty in the hospital room the night before the surgery.
The morning of the surgery, Marty's blood pressure was measured at 46 beats per minute. It was a testimony to the peak conditioning he'd worked himself into. As he was wheeled into the operating room, Marty had a surprise in store for the team of surgeons that would perform the surgery.

"They told me to be naked under my gown. As a joke I had on a pair of Halloween underwear. Everyone in the room broke into laughter and relaxed a bit," Marty explained.

For eight hours the surgeons operated on Marty, while Rob nervously waited back in his own room. Two-thirds of Marty's liver was removed and then Rob was brought in and the surgeons removed his diseased liver before transplanting his brother's donated organ into him.

The next thing that Marty can remember is the doctors calling for him to wake-up. Because he'd been under anesthesia for so many hours, there was a real chance that he might not be able to be revived.

"It was like crawling out of a deep, dark hole," Marty said. "I could hear them calling, but it took all of my effort to finally pry my eyes open."

The surgery was a success. The medical team explained that Rob's liver was so diseased that he probably wouldn't have survived more than a few more days if he hadn't had the surgery. A strange fact about liver donations is that the recipient recovers almost immediately with little pain, while the donor faces a months-long recovery fraught with searing pain.

The first question both Giles boys asked upon waking from surgery was, "How's my brother?" After being discharged from the hospital Marty and Rob went back to their parents' home and spent the next several months recovering together. Rob showed improvement almost immediately and has since returned to full health.

"To see my brother today, he has a good job and a wonderful girlfriend, and to know that I was able to help save my best friend is a feeling that I cannot put words to," Marty said.

A surgeon might explain that Marty Giles saved his brother Rob's life by giving him 66% of his liver, but a poet knows that Rob Giles is alive today because his brother gave him 100% of his heart.

*To learn more about the living donor program contact:*
*Cleveland Clinic, 9500 Euclid Avenue, Cleveland, OH 44195, 1.800.223.2273 ext. 42200*
*http://www.clevelandclinic.org*

# Firefighters Play Santa To Bring Christmas To Hundreds Of Area Kids

*For little children everywhere*
*A joyous season still we make;*
*We bring our precious gifts to them,*
*Even for the dear child Jesus' sake*
–Phebe Cary.

Firefighters have always been held in the highest regard by the people of the communities where they serve. Aside from risking their lives saving folks from fires, floods and accidents, the men and women of the fire department are often the first ones thought of when a non-fire emergency arises. Whether it's an elderly person who has fallen and can't get up or a frightened kitten stuck in a tree, the local fire department is always there to save the day.

If you spend any time around a fire hall and the people who inhabit it, one word will keep coming back to you over and over – compassion. Much like the healthcare profession, the battle against the out-of-control version of man's greatest invention, fire, calls out to people who have an innate desire to help their fellow man.

It should not surprise you then, that this next story finds its seeds in one fireman's desire to help the children of his community.

His name was Leo F. Heck, and in the 1920s he was one of Niagara Falls' top firemen. It was a common occurrence, in Leo's days, for people to drop off old toys that needed repair as a type of donation to needy families.

"Why not make a toy fund out of it and solicit donations of toys, new or used, to help make Christmas more merry for impoverished kids?" asked Leo.

So, in 1929, the first annual Niagara Falls Firefighter Toy Fund was held. For decade after decade folks donated new or used toys and the firefighter volunteers made any repairs that were necessary and saw that they made their way to kids who might otherwise be greeted by a bare Douglas Fir come Christmas morning.

In the 1970s, the toy fund got a shot in the arm from the fledging cable company in Niagara Falls, operated by the Laurendi family. As a result of the TV exposure the toy fund was catapulted into the modern era that most Niagara County residents know and love.

On air personality Sal Paonessa started a wake-a-thon where he would stay on the air for 30 straight hours promoting solicitations for the toy fund. Soon thereafter, the toy fund became an annual two-day affair. With hosts such as Bob Koshinski, Blair McEvoy and Lou

Paonessa standing front and center, countless local music, dance and magic acts have been featured on the telethon and many area businesses have donated either money or goods and services to be auctioned off.

In January 2004, the current toy fund chairman, retired firefighter Bill Butski, discussed the many ways that the fund touches the community.

"Currently, we serve about 1,500 kids per year," Butski said.

"The kids come to us in a variety of ways. Sometimes they're referred by a social agency or one of the area schools. Other times it might be a private referral. We buy two toys for each child and deliver them to the parent(s) in time to be wrapped and placed under the Christmas tree."

Butski also told me how one day is set aside each year when kids in need of warm winter clothing are given certificates to shop for them at Wal-Mart.

Another big part of the toy fund, Butski explained, is the annual pre-Christmas dinner that the firefighters hold for approximately 500 senior citizens, most of whom are in assisted-care living facilities.

*(Courtesy of Frank Croisdale)*

*Niagara Falls Firefighter Brain LaRock prepares another load of presents.*

It was while talking about the dinner that Butski recounted for me an incident that brought a group of brawny, fearless firemen to tears.

"Many of the seniors who attend the dinner are in wheelchairs, " Butski Explained. "One year this man and woman were wheeled in separately and seated next to each other at one of the tables. They both had wedding bands on and were so happy to see one another. They spent the whole dinner holding hands. Later, I was standing with a group of about a half dozen firefighters when we were told that they were a married couple who live in separate nursing facilities. Nobody in the family ever took them to see each other and it was only by coming to our dinner that they had the opportunity to be together. Six guys who had seen the most unspeakable, tragic events stood there with tears in our eyes. If you didn't well up over that you might as well take your membership card to the human race and burn it right then and there."

"I can't say enough about Adelphia Cable (which purchased the cable company from the Laurendi Family)," Butski said. They have meant so much to this toy fund over the years.

This past year (2003) I was worried what would happen because they have consolidated everything out to West Seneca. Lou Paonessa (from the Programming and Community Affairs office in Niagara Falls) really went to bat for us. He got them to agree to put us on for one day, 12 hours, and to expand it to all of Adelphia's Western New York subscribers."

Paonessa had this to say about his association with the toy fund:

"I've always had a soft spot for the toy fund. Christmas is very important to my family and the work that they do is just so great."

Former toy fund chairman Blair McEvoy also sang the praises of the Laurendi family.

"My dad, who was a former mayor of Lewiston, used to say that 'you've got to put something back into the community where you work and where you live.' The Laurendi family went out of their way to do that by hosting the toy fund. We were on the air from 10 A.M. Saturday until 5 P.M. Sunday in the early years. It was a big commitment from a big-hearted family."

Butski, Paonessa and McEvoy gave almost identical answers to the question of what they hold most fondly of their association with the toy fund. Two responses came independently from each of the three men: The looks on the faces of both the seniors at the dinner and the parents of the kids receiving toys and the testimonials from people who have volunteered as adults who were once kids that received Christmas gifts from the toy fund.

McEvoy relayed a story to me that paints a most masterful picture of the generosity of the men and women who wear the uniform of a Niagara Falls firefighter.
"We used to get most of the toys from Jenss ( a Western New York institution now closed in Niagara Falls). There would be times when we'd get a frantic call on Christmas Eve that someone had found a family that had no money for Christmas gifts. Of course, the fund was already spent by that time. So, we'd pass the hat, call Jenss and they'd send someone down to open the store. We'd take a truck down and buy the toys and deliver them to the family."

There are many places in America where it's hard to identify the heroes. Not in Niagara Falls. They're the good guys in red hats that save Christmas for so many, each and every year.

*To find out more about the toy fund or to offer a donation, contact them at:*
*Niagara Falls Firefighters Christmas, Toy Fund, P.O. Box 271, Niagara Falls N.Y. 14304.*

# Carly's Club Gives Members New Hope In The Battle Against Cancer

*It is only with the heart that one can see rightly.*
*What is essential is invisible to the eye.*
–Antione de Sant-Exupéry

One of the best things that a kid can do is to join a club. The Boys and Girls Club provides a host of activities to keep kids off of the streets. The 4-H Club teaches kids about their role in helping maintain the delicate balance of nature. At school, kids can join science clubs, language clubs, glee clubs and even the Yorkers, to learn about the rich history of the Empire State.

The story that you are about to read concerns a young girl who, facing her own mortality, founded a club that has touched the lives of thousands of kids battling cancer. She was a kid who was handed more tough breaks than any 100 people should have to endure, and yet, she never dwelled on her problems, choosing instead to focus on finding solutions.

Her name was Carly Collard Cottone, and she founded Carly's Club for Kids and cancer research at Roswell Park.

The most difficult thing that a 3-year-old is supposed to have to deal with is the separation anxiety that accompanies the first day of pre-school. Saying good-bye to mommy and daddy, even for a few hours, is emotionally tough on a little one taking the first steps on the long road to getting an education.

Imagine then, the psychological trauma imposed on a young girl of that age having to say a permanent good-bye to her daddy.

Carly was just 2 1/2 when her dad, Tony, died suddenly and unexpectedly of lung cancer.

"He was one of the healthiest people I'd ever met," Chuck Collard explained. "He was a non-smoker, non-drinker, who ran three to five miles daily. He died just four days after seeing a doctor. We were all in shock."

Just three years later, fate would again play a cruel joke on five-year-old Carly.

"Carly's mom, Judy, was my aunt. Because there were only seven years between us, we had always been more like sisters," Chuck's wife, CaroleAnn, who at different times in Carly's life had been the young girl's cousin, godmother and adoptive mother, explained. "Judy had been having headaches and went to the doctors. They told her that she had an inoperable brain tumor and gave her six months to live."

*( Courtesy of Jim Bush)*

*Carly Collard.*

Lightning, the wrong kind, had struck twice in little Carly's life. Judy wanted to be sure that Carly would be well taken care of and knew just the right people for the job. She came and asked Chuck and CaroleAnn Collard the most heart-wrenching question a parent could possibly ever have to pose. Would they take care of Carly then five-years-old?

"Carly had a bedroom in our home from the time she was born. She'd always been like a daughter to us. We were honored that Judy entrusted us with such a responsibility," CaroleAnn said.

"I work for Verizon and was all set to accept a promotion downstate. We were ready to move and I called and turned it down without hesitation that day. We knew that Carly was where she was supposed to be and that was right here with us," Chuck explained.

Judy was extremely courageous and battled for two years. Her tumor was a stage 4 when she was diagnosed and slowly robbed her of her ability to function normally.

"Judy visited Carly twice a week at the beginning. As she began to worsen, the visits tapered off. She didn't want Carly to see her like that. She told me, 'I don't want to bring her down. I want her to have a normal life.' She made the ultimate sacrifice for her daughter that she loved so much," said CaroleAnn.

In December of 1998, Judy Cottone lost her battle with brain cancer. Chuck and CaroleAnn were charged with the difficult task of explaining to seven-year-old Carly that both of her parents were now in heaven.

"I drove her to a place that we'd never been before because I didn't want her to have a bad association with somewhere she loved. I told her that her mom had passed away," Chuck explained.

Little Carly's response spoke volumes about how much the little girl had learned to distrust the permanence of keeping close the adults in her life.
"How old was my mom?" Carly asked Chuck.

"39."

"How old was my dad when he died?" Carly queried.

"39."

"How old are you?" she asked Chuck, who had to hold back tears as he connected the dots of her line of reasoning.

"I'm 32, sunshine, and I'm going to be here for a long, long time."

The Collards spent the next many months helping Carly adjust to life without her birth parents. CaroleAnn's training as a social worker for the Williamsville School District aided her in helping Carly to cope. The Collards began the procedure to formally adopt Carly.

For maybe the first time in her young life, things were finally going Carly's way.

(Author's note: The words that come next in this story have been, even from the safe distance of impartial retrospection, the most difficult that I've had to write. We all live by some unwritten rulebook that says that things will eventually even out. Endure the rain and the rainbow will be your reward. If anyone deserved a rainbow in her life, it was Carly Collard. And yet it was another unthinkable storm that would descend upon this little girl who had already lost so much to the rains.)

Just 10 months after her mother had passed, Carly began to have headaches. The Collards took her to see doctors who offered up a host of reasons to explain Carly's headaches.

"Sinus, migraines, stress in the form of a delayed reaction to Judy's passing, you name it and we heard it," CaroleAnn explained.

Finally the Collards insisted on a CAT scan. When doctors told them that Carly's medical insurance wouldn't pay for it, they offered to cover the cost out of their own pocket. The insurance eventually did cover the cost.

Carly had the CAT scan. Fourty-five minutes later, Carly's doctors at Sheridan Pediatrics called and told the Collards to bring her in right away.

Such calls never are a prelude to joyous news.

The doctors told the Collards words so surreal that they thought they must have been walking through a shared nightmare. "Carly has a brain tumor."

"I nearly fainted and got completely hysterical. Only when they told me that Carly could hear me from the next room did I calm down. I remember thinking, how can this be happening? How can a mother, father and child all get cancer within five years of one another?" CaroleAnn said.

When CaroleAnn phoned her mother in New Jersey to tell her the terrible news, her mom passed out and had to be taken to the hospital by ambulance.

Carly, a 3rd grader, just eight years old, was now in a fight for her own life with the same disease that had felled both of her parents. She underwent a ten-hour surgery at Children's Hospital in Buffalo, where doctors were confident that they'd removed the entire tumor.

It was while convalescing at Children's that Carly found herself perplexed at the disparity between the amount of items well-wishers had sent to her room and the lack of such things in the rooms of many other kids.

"People had sent her all types of toys, chocolates, necklaces, make-up and baskets from her school. Some people even sent money. When we walked the floor, Carly was deeply affected by the rooms where the kids had nothing. She immediately began to give her stuff away," Chuck explained.

The little girl, who had been stripped of so much of what we mistakenly take for granted, wanted nothing more than to share with others those things that she had been blessed with.

"She started asking, 'What else can we do?' and she said, 'Why don't we start our own group?' I asked her, 'What would you call it?' and she said, 'Carly's Club for Kids,'" CaroleAnn stated.

Carly immediately appointed herself "spokesperson" for Carly's Club and the organization began its pursuit of helping to find a cure for cancer while offering support to cancer patients and their families.

"We had no idea that Carly's Club would take off like it did. Four years ago, we would never have believed that it would impact every person that comes into Roswell," Chuck said.

"It began as a kids-helping-kids charity with a penny drive at Carly's school, Dodge Elementary. Today, with all of the corporate support we've received, it has become much larger then we'd ever dreamed imaginable," CaroleAnn added.

Throughout her battle with her illness, Carly never lost hope and she never lost her dignity. When chemotherapy robbed her of her beautiful hair, she proudly sported a colorful array of bandanas. She was very close to her brother, the Collard's son, Matthew. She wore a ubiquitous smile that warmed the hearts of everyone who aided her in her struggle to remain cancer-free.

After one year in remission, Carly's cancer returned very aggressively. A second surgery, a stem-cell transplant, was performed at Strong Memorial Hospital in Rochester. Afterward, Carly was hit with so much chemotherapy, her liver shut down. The Collards found out about a drug called Defibrotide that could help Carly. It was an experimental, non-FDA approved drug only available at three cancer centers including the Dana-Farber Institute in Boston. Carly was airlifted to Massachusetts and became just the 85th person and 11th child in the world to be treated with Defibrotide.

The Collard family spent the next four months living in a single room at the Ronald McDonald House in Boston. CaroleAnn was eight months pregnant before they left and had to be induced. Carly's second brother, Joshua, was born and the infant spent the first months of his life supporting his big sister in Beantown, while their brother, Matthew, attended the first grade in Boston.

After going through an amazing and unprecedented recovery, the Collards returned home and Carly got to go back to her normal life. Carly's friends at school had stayed connected to her while she was away by sending cards and greetings. A next-door neighbor took pictures of the middle school that Carly would be attending and mailed them to the young girl so she'd know what to expect. Carly was so glad to be back among her friends, going to school and having sleepovers.

On May 1st, 2002, Carly had another MRI. Within two hours, doctors called to say that the cancer had spread to her spine. At the end of June, Carly slipped into a coma resulting from a 106-degree temperature she experienced while battling pneumonia. She woke up on July 13th.

(Courtesy of Collards)

*The Collard family.*

"We always have a big 4th of July party," Chuck explained. "When she woke up, she asked what day it was. When I told her, she said, 'I missed the 4th of July party? Can we have a 4th of August party then?'"

On July 27th, the Collards celebrated a belated Independence Day by inviting 100 friends to their beach house. They rented a bounce house, played music, watched fireworks and celebrated an independence that a nation had found, but one that a courageous young girl would not.

On August 9th, Carly slipped into a coma and one week later, at the tender age of eleven, she passed away surrounded by the people she loved at her room at home.

Today, Carly's Club has become the sole fundraising arm of the pediatric unit of Roswell Park. Through a variety of fundraising efforts, the organization raised over $250,000 in 2003 and is approaching the $1 million mark overall for its three years in existence. Brian Moorman of the Buffalo Bills has become Carly's Club Honorary Spokesman.

Former Buffalo Sabre Rhett Warrener stills gives much of his time and efforts to the organization. Current Sabre J.P. Dumont stepped into the void created when Rhett was traded by offering $75,000 to purchase a Carly's Club suite for Sabres games. The suite is a place where cancer patients and their families can enjoy a few hours away from the world of doctors and treatments. During the 2003-2004 season, over 70 families attended games.

"People ask us, 'Where was God in all of this?'" CaroleAnn said. "God was in the family and friends who offered their prayers and support for Carly."

Those who knew her say that the reason that there are no pictures of Carly where she's not smiling is because her dictionary didn't include the word "frown."

You can honor this girl who weathered storm after storm and left the world a rainbow by joining her club and offering your help to find a cure for cancer once and for all.

"Carly touched the hearts of more people in eleven years then I ever will in 111," Chuck Collard said of his cherished daughter.

Carly Collard Cottone was taken from the world much too soon, but her smile, her hope and her legacy, in the form of Carly's Club For Kids, lives on. Someday researchers will find a cure for cancer and innocent children will no longer be at the mercy of this terrible disease. On that day, millions of us still left here on Earth will stand as one and we'll do what Carly so eloquently taught us to do.

We'll look to the heavens and we'll smile.

*To learn more about Carly's Club For Kids contact:*
*Carly's Club, Roswell Park Alliance Foundation, P.O. Box 631, Buffalo, NY 14240, 716-845-8788,*
*www.carlysclub.org*

# *WW II Vet Receives High School Diploma With Help From His Niece*

*The fireworks begin today. Each diploma is a lighted match.*
*Each one of you is a fuse.*
–Edward Koch

It was a common occurrence in Western New York in the early 1940s for a young man to leave school before graduating to heed Uncle Sam's call to join the fight "over there." Hitler and the Third Reich were threatening to put a stranglehold on Europe and American boys were saying "Goodbye Mother, hello General Patton."

Anthony Hunchar was one of those young men. In the spring of 1940, just one month shy of earning his high school diploma in Springville, NY, and just one year before the outbreak of WWII, he enlisted in the 12th Infantry Artillery Division. Manning anti-aircraft guns, Anthony was stationed in places as diverse as the Mojave Desert and Ascension Island.

After being discharged in 1945, Anthony returned home to Springville and married a lovely girl named Doris. Taking a job as the head custodian for the Springville School District, Anthony put in 31 years before retiring in March of 1983.

As the years blended one into the next, Anthony gave little thought to the sheepskin that was once almost within his grasp. In recent years his health began to fade and his family worried for his well-being. Anthony's niece, Lindsey Hintz, a freshman studying forensic science at West Virginia University, went to work to see that her great-uncle received something that had been owed to him for 64 years.

"My cousin Jackie graduated from Ellicottville High School in 2002 and during the ceremony a veteran came up and received his diploma," Lindsay explained. "I knew from my dad that my uncle never received his diploma and that's what prompted me to get the ball rolling."

Lindsay's dad, Dennis, challenged her with the statement, "What would happen if we helped get Uncle Tony his diploma?"
It was all the motivation that the spirited young woman needed.

"My first step was to interview my great-aunt Doris so that I had enough background information on my uncle. I didn't tell her what the interview was for because we wanted it to be a surprise for my uncle. It was kind of hard to keep it so secretive, but I'm glad that I did," Lindsay confided.

Lindsay then went on the Springville-Griffith Institute Board of Education Website and got a contact e-mail address.

"I wrote a detailed letter explaining who I was, who my uncle was and asked them to give him his diploma," Lindsay said.

Here is how she closed the letter to the school board:

The reason I am writing this letter is to ask if the Springville-Griffith Institute Board of Education would present my great-uncle with an honorary diploma. He served his time in the war fighting for our country, so that the freedom we enjoy now was preserved, then came back to put just as much devotion into his job as head custodian at the school he used to go to. Governor Pataki asked a few years back if the schools would honor war veterans who were not able to complete their schooling because they went to fight in the war. I know that his family and, most importantly, he himself would be very honored to receive a diploma that recognized him for his efforts.

*(Courtesy of Lindsay Hintz)*

**Anthony Hunchar receives his diploma as wife Doris looks on.**

I would ask that this could be done soon because of his failing health. I know that he would be greatly honored by this.

Lindsay received a letter back from the board saying that they'd be delighted to present Anthony with his diploma; all that was needed was his paperwork confirming his service in the war.

"I contacted his daughter, got the paperwork, and we were in business," Lindsay said.

The only formality left was to pick a date for the ceremony. Lindsay had hoped to be there to see her great-uncle receive his diploma in person, but her hectic out-of-state college schedule made that impossible.

Doris Hunchar explained the details as to how the evening was chosen.

"When they sent a letter and said that Tony was going to get his diploma, we were shocked. When we found out that Lindsay was the reason why, we wanted her to be there. We tried for a couple of different nights but they didn't work out. Finally her parents said to just go at the next opportunity, so we did."

And so it was on a February evening in 2004, during a Board Of Education meeting, that Anthony Hunchar, Class of 1940, was presented with his high school diploma.

Anthony doesn't mince words when asked how it felt to finally be recognized for work he had done as a young man.

"I was tickled pink," Anthony said.

"We never dreamed this could happen," added Doris.

As for Lindsay, she takes her achievement in getting her great-uncle recognized with a large dose of modesty.

"I only got the ball rolling, it was his life's achievements that were being honored. I'm just glad that I was able to play a part in making it happen."

Because of a young woman's love and appreciation for her great-uncle's personal sacrifice to heed the call of patriotism during the Second World War, Anthony Hunchar was blessed with an honor both revered and rare. The senior citizen for one night got to be a high school senior again and was bestowed with a new title to add to his life's resume – high school graduate.

*To learn more about the men and women who served during the Second World War, visit:*
*www.amvets.org*

# *Pavilion Boy Lives Life With A "Thumbs Up" Attitude*

*Hope, like the gleaming taper's light, adorns and cheers our way; and still, as darker grows the night, emits a brighter ray*
–Oliver Goldsmith

Imagine for a moment that you could again relive the twelfth year of your life. What if, instead of worrying about making the transition from grade to middle school, you had to deal with the trauma of learning that you had an incurable disease. You might think that a person in that position would wallow in self-pity and curse the hand that fate had dealt him. Would it stretch the limits of believability to think that a young man could receive such news and put aside his own suffering to use the rest of the time that he had remaining on Earth to better the lives of other children? If you think that to be so, you won't after reading the story that follows of a boy who left behind a legacy of love and compassion that continues to touch the hearts of people both near and far.

For the first 12 years of his life, John Clary was not unlike most kids. The grade-schooler from Pavilion, New York, lived in a nice home with his parents, Kevin and Rhonda, and his younger sister, Emily. John loved music and sports and the Clary home served as headquarters for a host of neighborhood kids. That John could have a major illness was the last thought to cross the Clarys' minds.

"The day before his 12th birthday, John said, 'Mom, my eyes feel funny,' I looked at his eyes and they looked fine," Rhonda Clary said as she and her husband Kevin sat in a conference room at the Pavilion High School. "The next day on his birthday, he didn't have any cake which I thought was really odd."

"The next morning Kevin had left for work and I was getting ready for work myself (Rhonda is a teacher at the high school). The dog kept coming in and out and wanted me to follow her. When I did I found John on the kitchen floor," Rhonda explained.

At first Rhonda thought that her son was playing a practical joke on her. When she realized that he was really unconscious, she told John's sister, Emily, to dial 9-1-1. John was rushed by ambulance to a hospital in Batavia.

"I actually beat the ambulance there," Kevin said. "The doctors told us John had had a seizure. His pediatrician was right next door and we explained to her what happened. She recommended that we see the neurologists at Golisano Children's Hospital at Strong in Rochester, NY."
The doctors did a CAT scan and an EEG and diagnosed John with a mild form of epilepsy. John was put on an anti-seizure medication and did well for a few months.

"We went on our annual trip to South Bend, Indiana, to see the Notre Dame football team play. We were in a store and I looked behind me and John wasn't there. I retraced my steps and when I went around a corner, there was John on the ground having another seizure. He didn't want me to tell his mother," Kevin explained.

Rhonda contacted the Epilepsy Foundation and began doing her own research about epilepsy. One of the things she read was that an MRI was recommended. Doctors believed that they could learn more from an MRI than from a CAT scan or EEG so Rhonda asked John's neurologist to order a MRI.

*(Courtesy of Clarys)*

**John Clary.**

On a Friday night, John had the MRI. On Saturday morning, doctors broke the news to the Clarys that John had a brain tumor. On Monday morning, John underwent surgery at Golisano Children's Hospital at Strong Memorial to remove as much of the tumor as was possible.

The doctors were able to remove about 30% of the tumor. The rest proved too effusive, as the spider-like tumor, that appeared much like spilled milk on the MRI, was just too difficult and too small to get at. The surgeons told the Clarys that the tumor was probably benign, but that they wanted to send out part of it for more testing.

Several weeks later, the biopsy test results came back and the Clarys had some frightening new words added to their vocabulary – Gliomatosis Cerebri (GC). What was known of John's condition was from research done in the early 1980s. GC was very rare in adults and almost nonexistent in children. In John's case, the tumor was primarily located in the right temporal lobe part of his brain. Before the advent of MRI technology, most diagnoses were made only at an autopsy. In an instant, the security that comes from the enjoyment of good health was ripped away and the Clarys found themselves facing some difficult decisions.

John, who was an active member of the Boy Scouts, had a Pinewood derby scheduled for the day when he learned he needed surgery. He was very upset about having to miss that and go into the hospital.

"We had a family meeting and all hugged one another and just decided that we would get through it together," Kevin said.

When John went home from the hospital he displayed the first ounce of what would prove to be an almost limitless supply of resolve, the type that would see him win over the hearts of hundreds of people throughout the region.

"They had shaved his head and he had a number of staples on his skull like a question mark," Rhonda said.

"I asked him, 'Do you want a scarf or something to cover it with?' And he answered, 'No, people will get used to it,'" Kevin told me.

John couldn't wait to get back to his regular life, a big part of which was his friends on the Pavilion Jr. High basketball team. He attended a game the morning after he came home from the hospital and would have suited up if his parents had let him.

The Clarys decided to celebrate every positive step that John took whenever possible. John drew from his own faith and was determined to do whatever he had to do to get rid of the tumor.

"We met with the radiation people and they recommended some focus radiation and then some overall radiation. In other words, they said, we'll hit the big parts first and then hit it overall because the tumor was everywhere in John's brain," Kevin confided.

"They said then that they were running along this fine line of giving him enough radiation to do something and too much where he could become a vegetable," Rhonda said. "What made us feel better was that they consulted with doctors at Duke University and elsewhere and decided that this was the best course of action."

"We asked if we were in the best place for John because we were ready to take him wherever he would get the best care. They told us that, due to the Internet and the ability to communicate almost instantly, he would get the same care here as he would anywhere," Kevin added.

"On his 13th birthday, we rented a limo for the ride to the hospital. We had cake, that John himself had baked, and a little party. Even though they told us that day that John would need a couple more weeks of treatment we still enjoyed the moment," Kevin said.

Earlier, doctors had pulled Kevin and Rhonda aside and told them that the tumor would be difficult to treat and may not respond to the radiation treatment. Fearing that his 13th birthday might be his last, the Clarys rented the local fire hall and threw John a huge bash.

"He always loved big gatherings and loved to be around adults, sometimes more than he did kids his own age. In his mind he was an adult and he had a great time at that party," said Rhonda .

In June of that year, John began a yearlong session of chemotherapy. During this time his weight dropped from 130 down to 87 pounds. Most of John's hair was already gone from the radiation.

"John rewrote a lot of chapters in the medical books. He wasn't supposed to live past 13 and he did, medicines that were supposed to make him nauseous didn't and ones that they thought wouldn't have much of an effect helped him greatly. It got to the point where I was telling the doctors, 'Hey, this is John Clary, things aren't going to be what you think they will when it comes to him,'" Kevin said.

That fall the Clarys traveled back to Notre Dame and a friend of Kevin's arranged for them to meet with Head Football Coach Bob Davie. The coach gave the family a whirlwind tour of the campus where they got to meet the players and go on the field at the stadium. The Clarys were even invited into the sanctity of the Notre Dame locker room after the game.

"Coach Davie was just phenomenal. To do what he did for John is something that I will never forget," Kevin stated.

The generosity of the football community wouldn't end at the collegiate level for the Clarys during that trip.

"John had met a counselor from Camp Good Days and Special Times who invited him to a Green Bay Packers game. We said, 'What the heck,' and went on up to Wisconsin. We got the royal treatment from the Packers. John met Brett Favre and all the guys. Reggie White even said a prayer with him." Kevin explained. "On the plane ride home, he was throwing up in a bag from the chemo, but he wouldn't have missed that trip for anything."

Throughout his ordeal, John missed very little school. He loved the social aspect of school and thrived on staying in contact with all of his friends and teachers. By the time he reached high school in 9th grade, most of John's friends were too uncomfortable with his illness or were busy with their own activities or sports to come to his home. The one exception was John's best friend, Russell Fanton, who continued to visit John. Russell and his family loved John as one of their own and regularly took him with them when they went out to eat or for other social functions.

During the time of his treatments, John also needed to wear a taekwondo type of helmet to protect his head should he fall as the result of a seizure. He was still having several seizures a day. John loved small children and feared that they might become fearful of the way he looked wearing the helmet. He would take the time to explain why he wore the helmet and get down on his hands and knees so that they could feel it and not fear him.

At Golisano Children's Hospital at Strong Memorial, John became an ambassador for the institution, taking it into his own hands to greet sick kids who were there for treatment.

"We heard stories that he'd go right up to the kids and say, 'Hi, my name's John. Don't be afraid, the doctors here are great and I'll show you where everything is," Rhonda explained.

Rochester radio station Mix 100.5 started a radiothon to raise funds for Golisano Children's Hospital at Strong Memorial. John was invited to the inaugural broadcast and became an immediate fixture at the annual affair. Because of his gregarious nature, John was a natural behind the microphone and became almost a third anchor for the broadcast.

Said Mix 100.5 Program Director Dave LeFrois of John:

*At our Radiothon every year, John was always there offering to help. And not just for an hour or two. He'd stick with us for hours and hours, day after day. Sometimes he'd answer phones on the volunteer phone bank, other times he'd join us on the air to talk about his illness and encourage listeners to call with a pledge.  We loved having him around.*

*I met him at our first Radiothon in 2000 and I quickly realized that whenever we put him on the air, the phones would start ringing like crazy.  He came across on the radio as a polite, positive, and caring young man -- and he clearly connected with our listeners.  He'd talk about his illness, his everyday challenges, and his fears and hopes, and he did it in such a strong, confident, matter-of-fact way that he seemed to approach a brain tumor in the same way most kids would approach a slightly challenging homework assignment.*

*John seemed fascinated by our line of work.  When we weren't interviewing other kids or families, we'd invite him to put on a set of headphones and join us at the broadcast table. That's the image of him that I'll never forget. He sat there with us, microphone in hand, always ready and able to take part in the conversation. He truly became a part of our team. We were always impressed with his attitude, his intelligence, and his sense of humor. Other kids his age might have dismissed a radio station that caters to his parents' generation. But he was always so respectful.*

*Over the years we kept in touch with John and his family, and every year they'd show up at the Radiothon and spend practically every minute of every day at the event -- answering phones, supervising the phone bank, assisting with administrative tasks, etc.  Seeing his commitment to helping others made us feel that much stronger about our commitment. Here he was fighting this awful illness that made him suffer unpredictable and frightening seizures, and in all those years we never once heard him complain about it.  He was there to help the hospital.  Four days of live broadcasts can take their toll on a person, but whenever any of us started to complain about sore feet or aching backs, we quickly realized how dumb we sounded.*

*John died just two weeks before our fifth Radiothon, which we dedicated to him.  At our broadcast table, between our two on-air hosts, we placed an empty chair as a tribute and a reminder.  We felt his absence, but we also felt his spirit.  And he made the phones ring.*

In his junior and senior years of school, John had to deal with frequent seizures, side effects of his medicines and steroids, and yet another round of chemotherapy. This combination caused fatigue, nausea, dramatic weight gain and osteoporosis that forced John to use a wheelchair. But, once again, John's faith and determination came into play. John wanted to make sure he did what his classmates were doing. He went to homecoming dances and proms and other school activities. He wanted his life to be as normal as possible.

John loved music and he especially wanted to remain in the senior high chorus as long as he could. Prior to his need for the wheelchair, John would sometimes have a seizure and fall down during concert performances. But John had made an arrangement with his friend Russ Fanton that, if he fell, Russ would help John back to his feet once the seizure had passed. John would then steady himself on his feet and continue on with the song. He didn't want any special attention.

John also asked that he be able to continue to participate in a team sport of some type. With the help of several wonderful coaches, John was able to join the track team and compete in the discus and shot put. He tried his best at each event to improve his personal best. At one track meet he even got to "run" the final leg of a 400-meter relay in his wheelchair.

John graduated with his high school class and received several awards and honors at the commencement. He was assisted onto the stage in his wheelchair, but when it came time to receive his diploma, he stood and walked across the stage.

That summer he began attending Happiness House, which specializes in training and life-skills programs for adults with brain injuries.

At around the same time, the Clarys learned that John's tumor was growing again and that another round of chemo was needed. John responded to this news by declaring, "Bring it on."

In November of 2003, shortly after starting the chemo, John was admitted into Golisano Children's Hospital at Strong Memorial and slipped into a coma-like state for two weeks. The Clarys prepared for the worst.

*(Courtesy of Clarys)*

***John with souvenirs from his visit with the Green Bay Packers.***

On Thanksgiving Day, John would give his parents something to be truly thankful for - he woke up. By mid-December, John had progressed enough to want to go home. On Christmas Day, the Clarys received the present of John's discharge from the hospital. John said that coming home was the best present he could have received.

John felt well enough to return to Happiness House and he went back to his program for a short period. By February, however, John alarmed his parents by declining to go to the program one day, something he had never done before.

"Even near the very end, when he could barely hold his head up, the doctors suggested that there were some options, but that they could put his life in danger. John, as weak as he was, managed to give his "thumbs up" sign. His attitude still was, 'Let's do it, let's go forward full steam ahead,'" Kevin explained.

On February 13, 2004, John Clary passed away peacefully. The outpouring of love for the young man who had touched so many surprised even Kevin and Rhonda.

"We knew that he touched a lot of people, but we had no idea how many," Rhonda said.

"When we drove to the church for his funeral, I'd never seen so many cars in Pavilion before," Kevin added.

Later that day, the Pavilion High School opened the auditorium for a remembrance for John. Several students and teachers walked to a microphone and told the audience how John had touched their lives.

The Clarys would receive another surprise when the 2004 Mix 100.5 Radiothon was dedicated to John's memory. When Kevin went down to the broadcast, he was rendered speechles when he saw that an empty chair had been placed between the two hosts that had a nameplate reading "In Loving Memory of John Clary" engraved on it.

John once wrote a paper for school entitled "The Tumor." Ostensibly, the protagonist of the story is a middle-aged man named "Brett Claremont," but the piece really was an autobio-graphical account of John's diagnosis and treatment for his brain tumor.

John closes the story with words given to him by another cancer survivor. The piece is called "Keep Fighting" and it tells you all that you need to know about the heart of John Clary.

### Keep Fighting

**One of the most difficult things everyone has to learn is that for your entire life you must "keep fighting" and adjusting if you hope to survive. No matter who you are or what your position, you must you must keep fighting for whatever it is you desire to achieve.**

**If someone is not aware of this contest and expects otherwise, then constant dis-appointment occurs. People who fail sometimes do not realize that the simple answer to everyday achievement is to keep fighting.**

**Health, happiness and success depend upon the fighting spirit of each person. The big thing is not what happens to us in life - but what we do about what happens to us.**

Kevin and Rhonda Clary miss John every day, but feel proud and fortunate to have been the parents of such a fine young man. Emily will miss not having her brother around, but she will always remember him. In the meantime, those of us left on Earth can draw strength from John Clary's example and meet the difficulties in our own lives with a recipe that's equal parts love, faith, determination and a "thumbs up" attitude.

*To learn more about the organizations that mattered most to John Clary, visit:*
*www.stronghealth.com/about/hospitals/gch.cfm, www.campgooddays.org*

# *Genesee County Boy Lives Real-Life "Rudy" Moment*

*For when the One Great Scorer comes to write against your name, He marks - not that you won or lost - But how you played the game.*
*–Grantland Rice*

It's no mere coincidence that this story follows the one that you've just read about John Clary. The heroics that you will learn about happened just four days after John passed away, inside the same high school that he attended. The boy you're about to meet, Teddy Schwytzer, was John's friend. The two boys were teammates on the Pavilion High track team. A week that began so tragically for the Pavilion High student body would end on a high note to lift everyone's spirits.

Teddy Schwytzer is the type of kid who isn't shy around adults. On the day that I was to interview Teddy along with his parents, D.G. and Peg, and Pavilion basketball coach Rob Milligan, I arrived at the school early. There were a group of boys hanging around near the school's gymnasium and one of them spotted me and walked over.

"Are you the guy here to talk to me for a book?" the kid asked.

"Yes," I answered. The kid thrust out his hand.

*(Courtesy of Carlson Studio)*
**Teddy Schwytzer.**

"Nice to meet you, I'm Teddy."

Later, after Teddy's parents and coach arrived, we sat around a conference table and I learned much more about the amazing 19-year-old with Down Syndrome who had served as team manager for the Pavilion boy's basketball team for the past four years.

"Teddy always loved sports, as have I," D.G., a veterinarian, told me. "I guess it's natural to follow what your father does. We played baseball, soccer and basketball. Basketball is easy in the country because you just put a hoop at the end of the driveway and everyone can play."

At an early age, Teddy displayed a special love of basketball.

"At 6 o'clock in the morning before the school bus came, Ted would be out in the driveway shooting baskets," D.G. said.

Teddy's older brother, Andy, had played for the Pavilion team and Teddy wished for nothing more than to follow in his big brother's footsteps.

"Teddy tried out for the team as a freshman and didn't make it," Coach Milligan explained. "He wanted to be part of the team so much that we made him the manager, which he's been ever since."

Teddy took his duties as team manager very seriously. Whether it was passing out towels or yelling support to his teammates from the sidelines, Teddy embodied the adage that a job worth doing is a job worth doing well. As this would be Teddy's last year of eligibility for sports at Pavilion, there was a growing sentiment to get him off of the sidelines and into a game.

"It was a seed that was planted between the team and myself," Coach Milligan said. "I did some checking just to make sure that he was under the age requirements and had enough practices in and those sorts of things, then it was just a question of when."

Senior Night of 2004 seemed to be the perfect opportunity to get Teddy into a game. Not only was it the last home game for seniors, but the parents of the players would all be there as well.

| CALEDONIA-MUMFORD 75, PAVILION 47 | | | | |
|---|---|---|---|---|
| Caledonia-Mumford | 22 | 13 | 18 | 22 — 75 |
| Pavilion | 15 | 20 | 5 | 7 — 47 |

**CALEDONIA-MUMFORD:** Brian Pullyblank 22, Paul Keeley 6, Chris Chiverton 7, Steve Burns 8, Brett Shaffer 7, Aaron Hallett 6, Justin Walsh 10, Chris Harmon 3, Rick Riggi 2, Zack Nothnagle 2, Jeff Grattan 2.
**PAVILION:** Mitch Robinson 11, Jed West 2, Chris Logsdon 4, Matt Cerefin 2, Scott Noble 6, Gerry Harris 2, Brent Heywood 10, Brad Archibald 0, Kenny Quackenbush 0, Brian Galliford 3, Jack McCulley 5, Jason Erbach 0, Teddy Schwytzer 2.
**3-pointers:** Pullyblank, Shaffer, Chiverton, Hallett 2; Galliford, Heywood 2, Robinson.
**Fouled out:** none.

*Box score showing teddy's basket.*

"Teddy asked me, very early in the season when Senior Night was. He was really excited that his parents would be introduced and that he'd get to hand flowers (a school tradition) to his mother," said Coach Milligan.

Pavilion's opponent for the game was Caledonia–Mumford. Coach Milligan explained his wishes to get Teddy onto the court to Cal-Mumford coach Dan Dickens, who was all for the idea. The plan was to get Teddy into the game no matter the score, a decision that was made easier after Cal-Mumford pulled away in the second half after the teams had entered halftime tied at 35 apiece.

"I'm glad that I didn't have to make the decision of whether to put Teddy in if the game had stayed close. I was committed to put Teddy in regardless of the score. The crowd was really loud and had been calling for me to put him in most of the second half. I don't think I would have made it out of there alive if I didn't put him in," Coach Milligan explained.

There were about three minutes remaining when Teddy hit the hardwood and his teammates immediately began feeding him the ball. Teddy launched, and just missed, a few three-point attempts.

There's an old saying in basketball – shooters shoot. Teddy, a shooter by nature, kept firing up jumpers. Just when it seemed like Teddy might miss out on his dream of reading his name in the next day's box score, an ending seemingly written by a Hollywood screenwriter materialized.

Teddy drove to the basket and put up a lay-up that rolled off of the rim. One of his teammates, a young man from South Africa new to the game of basketball, put up, and missed, three straight shots.

Now, you hear a lot about the poor state of today's youth. Kids are often thought of as selfish, lazy and lacking compassion. What happened next on the court should provide even the most vocal of critics with a restored confidence in the innate goodness residing inside America's children.

Cal-Mumford center Rick Riggi – at 6'4", the tallest kid on the court – rebounded the ball and handed it to the shortest kid in the game – Teddy. It is a testimony to Riggi's character that he was able to recognize the magnitude of the moment and display such compassion for one of his opponents. For a moment, Teddy was so surprised at the gesture that he started to head down court to play defense. When he realized that he had the ball, Teddy stopped and fired a sweet shot in off of the glass that was true from the moment it left his hands.

The crowd erupted in thunderous applause and Teddy pumped his fist in celebration. If you can imagine the climactic scenes in "Rudy," "Hoosiers" and "Remember the Titans" all rolled into one, you'll begin to have an understanding of the emotional impact of the moment on all of those lucky to be present.

*(Courtesy of Pavilion Central School - Linda Deval)*

**The Pavilion High boys basketball team 2004.**

"It was indescribable. It just didn't seem real, like it was a dream," Peg Schwytzer said of witnessing her son's amazing shot. Teddy's brother, Andy, was on hand to witness the feat, while his sister Emily, who was studying abroad in London for a semester, learned of Teddy's heroics during a joyous transatlantic phone call.

"How did you feel when you sank the shot?" D.G. asked Teddy.

"Pretty good, pretty good," was his modest reply.

Since the game and all of the media coverage that followed, Teddy's teammates have given him a new nickname, Sweetness. It is most fitting because his special moment in the spotlight sent a crowd of people home brimming with the euphoric sensation of unbridled sweetness.

"I played basketball here and I'm sure that we had a Senior Night, but I couldn't tell you a thing about the game," D.G. said. "These kids will always remember their Senior Night, that's for sure."

Teddy Schwytzer gave the people of Pavilion a moment that they'll never forget. As the crowd was serenading Teddy with cheers, somewhere John Clary was looking down on his friend. You can bet John was also cheering.

*To learn more about the Genesee Area Special Olympics, contact:*
*Special Olympics New York - Genesee Region, 1 Grove Street, Suite 216, Pittsford, NY 14534.*
*(585) 586-7400, http://www.nyso.org/genesee.php*

*Visit the Pavilion High School online at: www.Pavilioncsd.org*

# *For The Wife Who Has Given Me Everything – Happy Valentine's Day*

*Oh, if it be to choose and call thee mine,*
*Love, thou art every day my Valentine!*
–Thomas Hood

February 14 marks the celebration of the most romantic day of the year, Valentine's Day. Of course, for many men it is also a time of considerable anxiety, as women expect an impassioned day that will outdo what has been done before.

It is in just such a predicament that I find myself as the day when we honor the patron saint of love quickly approaches. My wife and I will celebrate five years of wedded bliss this August. We have a two year-old child, a house, a dog, a cat and two cars. In short, the American dream. As is not uncommon with today's couples, we are often so caught up in the daily ritual of juggling family and career that romance is often strapped into the last seat on the caboose and forgotten.

How then can I show this woman who embodies the phrase "better half" that without her daily love and support I'd be little more than another nicked piece of china on the clearance shelf of life?

Maybe a search of the holiday's origins would be a good jumping-off point?

The most popular legend is that Valentine was a priest in third-century Rome. Emperor Claudius II came to the decision that soldiers performed better on the battlefield if their heads weren't filled with images of wives and children back home, so he outlawed marriage for all defenders of Rome. This decree didn't sit too well with Valentine, who defied it by continuing to perform marriages. It is said that Valentine was imprisoned and put to death for his actions. Many believe that before Valentine was executed, he fell in love with the beautiful young daughter of his jailer. She visited him often during his confinement and, as a last act on this earth, he wrote her a letter professing his eternal love and signed it "from your Valentine."

A cynic might say that old Valentine would have been better off just minding his own business, leaving the affairs of the heart to the world outside the priesthood. A romantic, on the other hand, would argue that, had Valentine not followed his heart, he would never have found his soul mate before leaving this plane forever.

All of it interesting, but not necessarily helpful in my quest to profess my love for my wife on the grandest scale imaginable. Is it enough to say that we have a love to die for? Sure, we bicker and grouse the way married couples do, but that's just mere window-dressing on the great department store that is our life. In the main showroom are two wagons, tightly circled against all outside threats. We are an original posse of two and if I could lift the limitations of the medium we are currently using, I would illustrate our love with gangsta hand signals that spell out "Frank- N-Dawn, 4-Life."

Just the fact that you're reading these words now has as much to do with her love as it does with my abilities. She was the first woman in my life who ever really, truly, from the depths of her heart encouraged my writing and pushed me to follow my bliss. She convinced me that stringing words together for the printed page was my gift and that my voice was needed in our community and in this world. Is that a debt that can be repaid with a bouquet of roses?

*(Courtesy of Dawn Croisdale)*

*Valentines Day 2004.*

Can a mere box of chocolates convey to her the way she can still melt my heart with her smile? Could any confectionery be as sweet as her kiss or as comforting as her embrace? Yes, life may be like a box of chocolates, but at least I know that whatever surprises come my way, I won't have to face them alone.

Is there any verse in the Hallmark universe to tell my wife how proud I am of the mother that she is to our son? What couplet could sing her my gratitude for her patience with our little boy that I as a father often lack? She who once threw herself down a flight of stairs without hesitation to prevent our son from toppling over backward, only later realizing that she was bruised and cut from the exploit. Is there a fancy card on the shelves to say thanks for that?

It's not always the biggest, most obvious, things that define love, but the little nuances that are noticed just by the two of you. How can I express to the love of my life how much it blew me away when we were first dating and I realized that she knew the words to every song by the Beatles? Without her, I might still be oblivious to the music of Nanci Griffith, School of Fish and the Blackhawks. Music is the soundtrack to the soul and she has added so much to the score of mine.

Her appreciation of art does not begin and end with music. How can I tell her that I admire her dedication to reading and her innate talent for decorating? How can I show my admiration for her achievement in rising above the mentality of the crowd she hung with as a young woman, becoming the only one among them to put herself through college? She downplays her bachelor's degree in psychology from the University of Buffalo, treats it as if it were something that was won in a sweepstakes drawing, when it speaks volumes about her character and perseverance. Would a fancy dinner at John's Flaming Hearth illustrate my awe for that part of her being?

I could hire an airplane to write her name in the sky, but it wouldn't capture one iota of her best attribute, her laugh. Her laugh is bold where she is not. It is boisterous where she is meek. It walks on water where she refuses to dip even a temperature-testing toe beneath the surface.

I defy anyone to hear my wife laugh and resist the urge to join in her merriment. One might fare better resisting the urge to sing with sirens or dance with fairies. Tell me, how do I thank her for the countless times that her laugh has saved me from myself? I don't think a goblet full of "Be Mine" or "Love Me" candy hearts will suffice.

Rest assured that I will shower my love with roses on Valentine's Day and I'll probably throw in some sweet chocolate, too. I'll offer a card steeped in deep reds and coy pinks.
But none of those things will even scratch the surface in telling my wife, Dawn, how much her love means to this simple man. I think that I could live a million lifetimes and still not find the right words to string together to truly convey those thoughts.

Maybe reading this will be a start. That and this hopeful request:

*Will you be my Valentine?*

# *About The Author*

Frank Thomas Croisdale is a Contributing Editor for the *Niagara Falls Reporter*. His weekly column is syndicated by the Sample News Group for their flagship newspaper the *Corry Journal*.

Frank's work has led to numerous radio and television appearances, including a spot as a guest panelist on MSNBC's *Scarborough Country*.

*(Courtesy of Dawn Croisdale)*

Frank has donated his time to many charitable causes and was co-founder of the SEA of Niagara Campaign to benefit the Aquarium of Niagara. He also has helped many in his community as a member of the Disaster Action Team of the American Red Cross.

Frank is a former Vice President of Sales for Gray Line of Niagara Falls. For many years he has owned his own company, *Niagara Falls Help & Information Services*, promoting the attractions and accommodations of Niagara Falls, New York and Ontario. He is currently the tour sales director for Niagara's premiere hotel, the Niagara Hilton.

He and his wife Dawn live with their son, Ryan, in Appleton, New York.

Do you know of a story that can be considered a Buffalo Soul Lifter? If so, you can send your idea to Frank Thomas Croisdale at:
>          Western New York Wares
>          P.O. Box 733
>          Ellicott Station
>          Buffalo, NY 14205

# *Birth of a Publishing Company*

The Buffalo area's most innovative publishing company will celebrate its 21st anniversary in 2005 by hitting a benchmark that few regional publishing houses achieve. By that time, Western New York Wares Inc. will have moved about 195,000 books and other regional products into homes, schools and libraries around the world.

Think of it this way. If we laid all the books we've distributed cover-to-cover in a paper path starting at the foot of Main Street near HSBC Center, the trail would stretch beyond the UB South Campus, snake through Williamsville, pass Batavia and end about 20 miles outside of downtown Rochester. Putting it a different way, we've distributed more than 25 million pages of information about our region. We could hand out individual pages to every man, woman and child in New York State and still have enough pages to supply half the population of Pennsylvania!

A pretty impressive path for a company that sprouted its roots in trivial turf.

The year was 1984 and the trivia craze was taking the nation by storm. As Buffalo journalist Brian Meyer played a popular trivia game with friends in his North Buffalo living room, he envisioned a game that tests players' knowledge about people and events in their hometown. Western New York Trivia Quotient sold out its first edition in six weeks and established Meyer as an up-and-coming young entrepreneur.

A year later, he compiled a book of quotations that chronicled the feisty reign of Mayor Jimmy Griffin. Meyer refuses to disclose how many six-packs were consumed while sifting through hundreds of "Griffinisms."

Meyer, a City Hall reporter for the Buffalo News, spent 15 years at WBEN Radio where he served a managing editor. As founder and president of Western New York Wares Inc., Meyer has collaborated with dozens of authors, artists and photographers. By 2004, the region's premier publisher of local books had been involved in publishing, marketing or distributing more than 125 regional products.

The Buffalo native is a graduate of the Marquette University, St. Joseph's Collegiate Institute and Buffalo Public School #56. He teaches communications courses at Buffalo State College and Medaille College. Meyer is treasurer of the Greater Buffalo Society of Professional Journalists' Scholarship Fund.

Meyer is assisted by Michele Ratzel, the company's business manager, and Tom Connolly, manager of marketing and distribution. The trio has nearly half a century of cumulative experience in regional publishing. Connolly works as a news anchor and producer at WBEN Radio. He co-authored *Hometown Heroes: Western New Yorkers in Desert Storm.*

# *Other Regional Books*

Visit our Web site at *www.Buffalobooks.com* for a complete list of titles distributed by Western New York Wares Inc.

**Buffalo Memories: Gone But Not Forgotten** – The late George Kunz was blessed with a phenomenal memory. In his later years, he began chronicling his recollections of his Depression upbringing. For years, his anecdotes on everything from Bisons' games at Offermann Stadium to rides on the Canadiana and shopping excursions to 998 Broadway graced the pages of the Buffalo News. This book is a collection of about 200 of these anecdotes.
ISBN: 0-9671480-9-X                                                                                                          $15.00

**Beautiful Buffalo: Preserving a City** – Buffalo has been called one of the most beautifully planned cities in the nation. America's great architects, including Frank Lloyd Wright, Louis Sullivan and Stanford White, helped make our city what it is today – a mecca for preservation pilgrims. Linda R. Levine and Maria Scrivani collaborated on a project that includes archival and contemporary photographs of many sites.
ISBN: 0-9740936-2-9                                                                                                          $19.95

**Victorian Buffalo: Images From the Buffalo and Erie County Public Library** – Visit Buffalo as it looked in the 19th century through steel engravings, woodcuts, lithography and other forms of nonphotographic art. Author Cynthia VanNess has selected scenes that showcase everyday life and views of historic structures created by luminaries like Frank Lloyd Wright, Louis Sullivan and E.B. Green.
ISBN: 1-879201-30-5                                                                                                          $13.95

**Frank Lloyd Wright's Darwin D. Martin House: Rescue of a Landmark** – The untold story of the abandonment and rescue of the region's most architecturally-significant home is recounted in vivid detail by Marjorie L. Quinlan. The book includes color photos and detailed architectural plans.
ISBN: 1-879201-32-1                                                                                                          $13.95

**National Landmarks of Western New York: Famous People and Historic Places** – Gracious mansions and thundering waterfalls. Battleships and nostalgic fireboats. Power plants and Indian long houses. Author Jan Sheridan researched nearly 30 National Historic Landmarks in the Buffalo-Niagara and Finger Lakes regions. Dozens of photographs, maps and an index.
ISBN: 1-879201-36-4                                                                                                          $9.95

**Classic Buffalo: A Heritage of Distinguished Architecture** – A stunning hardcover book pays tribute to the region's architectural heritage. Striking full-color photographs by Andy Olenick and an engaging text by Richard O. Reisem make this coffee-table book a keepsake for history buffs.
ISBN: 0-9671480-06                                                                                                          $39.95

**Church Tales of the Niagara Frontier: Legends, History & Architecture** – This first-of-a-kind book traces the rich history and folklore of the region through accounts of 60 area churches and places of worship. Written by the late Austin M. Fox and illustrated by Lawrence McIntyre.
ISBN : 1-879201-13-5                                                                                                          $14.95

**Symbol & Show: The Pan-American Exposition of 1901** – A riveting look at perhaps the greatest event in Buffalo's history. Written by the late Austin M. Fox and illustrated by Lawrence McIntyre, this book offers a lively assessment of the Exposition, bringing to light many half-forgotten facts.
ISBN: 1-879201-33-X                                                                                                          $15.95

**Beyond Buffalo: A Photographic Journey and Guide to the Secret Natural Wonders of our Region** – Full color photographs and informative vignettes showcase 30 remarkable sites. Author David Reade also includes directions and tips for enjoying each site.
ISBN: 1-879201-19-4                                                                                                          $19.95

**Western New York Weather Guide** – Readers won't want any "winteruptions" as they breeze through this lively book written by former Channel 7 weather guru Tom Jolls. Co-authored by Brian Meyer and Joseph VanMeer, the book focuses on historic and humorous weather events over the past century.
ISBN: 1-879201-18-1                                                                                    $7.95

**White Death: Blizzard of '77** – This 356-page softcover book chronicles one of the region's most dramatic historical events. Written by Erno Rossi, the book includes more than 60 photographs.
ISBN: 0-920926-03-7                                                                                    $16.95

**Great Lake Effects: Buffalo Beyond Winter and Wings** – a unique cookbook that is filled with intriguing historical facts about the region. The hardcover book has been compiled by the Junior League of Buffalo.
ISBN: 1-879201-18-1                                                                                    $18.95

**Buffalo Treasures: A Downtown Walking Guide** – Readers are led on a fascinating tour of 25 major buildings. A user-friendly map and dozens of illustrations by Kenneth Sheridan supplement an enlightening text by Jan Sheridan.
ISBN: 1-879201-15-1                                                                                    $4.95

**Buffalo's Brush With the Arts: From Huck Finn to Murphy Brown** – A fascinating adventure behind the manuscripts and million-dollar book deals, highlighting the Niagara Frontier's connection to many creative geniuses. Authored by Joe Marren, the book contains more than 20 photographs from the Courier-Express Collection.
ISBN: 1-879201-24-0                                                                                    $7.95

**Uncrowned Queens: African American Women Community Builders of Western New York** – Historians Peggy Brooks-Bertram and Dr. Barbara Seals Nevergold celebrate the accomplishments of African American women. Some of them are well-known; others have not received previous recognition.
ISBN: 0-9722977-0-7                                                                                    $11.95

**Buffalo's Waterfront : A Guidebook** – Edited by Tim Tielman, this user-friendly guide showcases more than 100 shoreline sites. It includes a handy fold-out map. Published by the Preservation Coalition of Erie County.
ISBN: 1-879201-00-3                                                                                    $5.95

**The Rainbow City: Celebrating Light, Color and Architecture at the Pan-American Exposition, Buffalo 1901** – The story of Buffalo's glorious moment, recounted in 160 pages and more than 20 images. Written by Kerry S. Grant of the University at Buffalo, the book chronicles an era when Buffalo was the nation's eighth largest city.
ISBN: 0-9671480-5-7                                                                                    $15.00

**Game Night in Buffalo: A Town, its Teams and its Sporting Memories** – Our region has enjoyed a storied sporting history. Sal Maiorana's books stirs emotions and passions as he recounts many never-to-be forgotten games and performances that fans have cheered and cursed. Many photos accompany a riveting text.
ISBN 1-879201-44-5                                                                                    $12.95

**Tale of the Tape: A History of the Buffalo Bills From the Inside** – Eddie "Abe" Abramoski reflects on scores on humorous, emotional and enlightening anecdotes that stretch back to the first Bills training camp in East Aurora. Many photos accompany the lively text.
ISBN: 1-879201-41-0                                                                                    $10.95

**Bodyslams in Buffalo: The Complete History of Pro Wrestling In Western New York** – Author Dan Murphy traces the region's rich wrestling history, from Ilio DiPaolo and Dick "The Destroyer" Beyer, to Adorable Adrian Adonis. Dozens of photos.
ISBN: 1-879201-42-9                                                                                    $9.95

**Haunted Places of Western New York** – Mason Winfield, the region's most high-profile paranormal investigator and 21st century "ghosthunter," pens a first-of-a-kind guidebook. Readers learn about "spooky communities" in the area, encountering haunted inns, highways, colleges and theaters. There are even chapters that focus on battlefield ghosts and grave haunts.
ISBN: 1-879201-45-3                                                                                    $9.95

**Spirits of the Great Hill: More Haunted Sites and Ancient Mysteries of Upstate New York** – From Mark Twain's Buffalo ghost, to Houdini's Halloween, Mason Winfield pens a riveting sequel to his supernatural survey of the region.
ISBN: 1-879201-35-6                                                                                    $13.95

**Shadows of the Western Door: Haunted Sites and Ancient Mysteries of Upstate New York** – A supernatural safari across Western New York. Guided by the insights of modern research, author Mason Winfield pens a colorful, provocative and electrifying study of the paranormal.
ISBN: 1-829201-22-4                                                                                    $13.95

**A Ghosthunter's Journal: Tales of the Supernatural and the Strange in Upstate New York** – A delightfully diverse smorgasbord of strange encounters, all of them set in Western New York. The 13 fictional stories are inspired by the files of Mason Winfield.
ISBN: 1-879201-29-1                                                                                    $12.95

**The Erie Canal: The Ditch That Opened a Nation** – Despite its shallow depths, the waters of the Erie carry an amazing history legacy. It was in canal towns like Lockport and Tonawanda where the doors to the American frontier were unlocked. Written by Daniel T. Murphy, the book includes dozens of photos.
ISBN: 1-879201-34-8                                                                                    $8.95

**Goat Island: Niagara's Scenic Retreat** – Historian Paul Gromosiak explores the people, attractions, animals and plants that makes the islands above Niagara Falls a fascinating destination. The book includes color photos and a detailed map.
ISBN:  1-879201-43-7                                                                                   $9.95

**Nature's Niagara: A Walk on the Wild Side** – Learn more about the wild animals, plants and geological formations at Niagara Falls. Written by Paul Gromosiak, the book includes many full-color photographs and maps.
ISBN: 1-879201-31-3                                                                                    $8.95

**Daring Niagara: 50 Death-Defying Stunts at the Falls** – Paul Gromosiak pens a heart-stopping adventure about those who barreled, boated, even bicycled to fame. The book includes vintage photos.
ISBN: 1-879201-23-2                                                                                    $6.95

**Niagara Falls Q&A: Answers to the 100 Most Common Questions About Niagara Falls.** – Author Paul Gromosiak spent four summers chatting with 40,000 Falls tourists. This invaluable guide answers 100 commonly asked questions. The book also includes photos, many of them in color.
ISBN: 0-9620314-8-8                                                                                    $4.50

**Water Over the Falls: 101 of the Most Memorable Events at Niagara Falls** – Daredevils who defied the Mighty Niagara. Tragic rock slides and heroic rescues. More than 100 true-to-life tales are chronicled by local historian Paul Gromosiak. Color photos and vintage black-and-white photos.
ISBN: 1-879201-16-X                                                                                    $8.99

**Zany Niagara: The Funny Things People Say About Niagara Falls** – A lighthearted tour of humorous happenings and historical oddities. Penned by Paul Gromosiak and illustrated by John Hardiman.
ISBN: 1-879201-06-2                                                                                    $4.95

**Exploring Niagara: The Complete Guide to Niagara Falls and Vicinity** – Filled with 77 spectacular full-color photos, the guide includes dozens of wineries, canals, waterfalls and mansions. Authors Hans and Allyson Tammemagi also chronicle the history that shaped the region.
ISBN: 0-9681815-0-3                                                                                                    $14.25

**Niagara Falls** – One of the world's most spectacular natural wonders springs to life in a book that contains more than 150 color photographs. From a visit in 1678 when a missionary recorded the first eyewitness account of the Falls, to an autumn day in 1993 when Dave Mundy became the only person to survive two barrel rides over the Niagara, readers experience an exhilarating tour. The book includes chapters on the Gorge, Niagara-on-the-Lake, wineries, the famous floral clock and Fort Erie.
ISBN: 2-84339-023-0                                                                                                    $9.99

**The Magic of Niagara** – Viewing the Mighty Niagara for the first time stirs images of tranquility, power and magic. The story of Niagara is 12,000 years old, and author George Bailey skillfully captures the historical highlights in a book that contains a riveting text and more than 100 photographs. Sections include Niagara in the winter, the Maid of the Mist, famous daredevils and the Niagara Parks Butterfly Conservancy.
ISBN:  0-9682635-0-X                                                                                                  $15.99

**This is Niagara Falls** – Vibrant color photographs – more than 50 of them – capture the power and majesty of the Mighty Niagara. From the moment when darkness descends on this wonder and a dazzling display of lights appears, to the instant when the Maid of the Boat inches close to the foamy base of the Falls, this book captures the mystique of a this natural wonder.
ISBN:   1-879201-38-0                                                                                                 $7.98

**Toronto and Niagara Falls** – Two world-renowned destinations are showcased in one photo-packed book! More than 240 full-color photographs, a detailed street map, informative text and user-friendly index make this an invaluable companion.  Readers will explore Chinatown, museums, forts and gardens in Toronto. The Niagara Falls section highlights such attractions as Cave of the Winds and Maid of the Mist.
ISBN:   88-8029-569-1                                                                                                 $15.99